"Ever done it in the [...] Sam whispered

Cupping Jenna's face in his hands, he lowered his lips, teasing and tempting her with wispy, nipping bites. Her breathing quickened when his tongue snaked out and touched her mouth. What he tasted was rich, dark, forbidden.

Jenna's knees buckled and he caught her around the waist, holding her against his hard body. "Now, darlin'?" he murmured. "How about now?"

She didn't have time to respond as his mouth closed over hers. It was a shock to her that hunger could be so luscious. That it could taste so sweet. And then he stopped playing games and plundered her mouth, bruising it with a fervor that astounded Jenna to the depths of her soul, igniting a hot flood that she hadn't known she possessed. She met him, danced with him, in a honeyed waltz of desire and need.

Jenna dissolved into his sizzling touch, into his heady scent and harsh moans. She arched into him offering her own sigh of surprise. She tortured her fingers with the silky touch of his hair and partnered her tongue with his. And when she felt his hands drop to cup her breast, she knew that this was what the diaries had been all about.

Passion.

Dear Reader,

Promises are meant to be kept. That's what I was always taught. But keeping my promise has never proved to be a bigger challenge than the promise itself.

Jenna Sinclair promises her dying grandmother that she will retrieve her gran's damaging diaries. Though Jenna hadn't bargained for a sexy cowboy standing in her way. My, my, but even with that promise hanging over her head, she finds it hard to deceive Sam Winchester. All Jenna wants to do is throw caution to the wind and make hay with her irresistible cowboy. Ah, but that promise cannot be forgotten.

I hope you enjoy reading how Jenna and Sam stay true to themselves while giving in to their desires. I love to hear from my readers, so please write me at P.O. Box 1979, Centreville, Virginia 20122, or send me an e-mail at www.karenanders.com.

Enjoy!

Karen Anders

Books by Karen Anders

HARLEQUIN BLAZE
22—THE BARE FACTS
43—HOT ON HER TAIL

SILHOUETTE INTIMATE MOMENTS
780—JENNIFER'S OUTLAW

THE DIVA DIARIES

Karen Anders

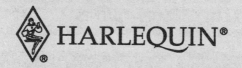

HARLEQUIN®

TORONTO • NEW YORK • LONDON
AMSTERDAM • PARIS • SYDNEY • HAMBURG
STOCKHOLM • ATHENS • TOKYO • MILAN • MADRID
PRAGUE • WARSAW • BUDAPEST • AUCKLAND

To Barbara,
The mother of my heart.
Thanks for being there when I need you.
(beep, beep, RR)

ISBN 0-373-79078-3

THE DIVA DIARIES

Copyright © 2003 by Karen Alarie.

Prologue

HIS HANDS WERE SMOOTH and hot against her bare shoulders.

The moment he touched her, the strains of a haunting aria wafted through her head, a piece she should know but couldn't identify, drifting over her like the gentle palms that played over her body.

Piercing blue eyes, strong jaw and a full, sensuous mouth were attributes that had caught her attention, but the man he was inside was the true prize.

His hands moved over her shoulders, gliding up to her face. His mouth was greedy when he kissed her, as greedy as she was for his kiss. And still the aria played in her head and he became part of the magic, twining and infusing the chords into solid limbs to hold her, hands to touch her, a heart to enfold her. In his arms, the music inside her came alive.

The dress slipped from her body, a glittering, shining treasure of silver and gold, pooling at her feet. She stepped out of it as easily as she vowed she would step away from the opera. Susanna Chandler would not look back.

Her hands pressed against the hard muscles of his chest. Her arms went around him to hold him close, like something precious once lost, now found. And she knew this was the perfect passion she'd searched for since her journey began.

She whispered his name.

He seemed to slip out of her grasp, his face swimming and indistinct. No, she fought against waking up. There was something she knew was there, something elusive, real...

"Gran. It's me."

"Jenna." Her granddaughter was petite with long, dark wavy hair. Her face mirrored perfect bone structure, her wide brown eyes almond-shaped, lined subtly in black with a shimmering rose eye shadow, her high, delicate cheekbones smooth, dusted with a muted dusky pink.

"Dreaming of Gramps again?" Jenna bent over the hospital bed, the scent of her exotic perfume familiar and welcoming to Susanna. Proud of the woman her granddaughter had become, Susanna offered up her cheek for a kiss. Smoothing down the rumpled sheet and blanket, Jenna sat in a chair beside the bed.

"Lately it's the same dream."

Jenna reached out and squeezed her hand. Turning to the nightstand, she picked up a glass and poured some ice water into it. Adding a straw, her granddaughter offered the cup to her. "You miss him, don't you?"

"Yes, immensely. He was the only man for me," Susanna said before she took a sip of the cold water.

"I miss him, too." When she held out the cup again, Susanna waved it away. Jenna set it back on the nightstand.

Susanna moved her frail hand and clasped her

granddaughter's. Her other one clasped a small ruby-red book and something infinitely more precious.

When Susanna had been young, she had wanted to experience all that life had to offer. But unlike her, Jenna retreated and hid in the shadow of her music, convinced that was all she really wanted. It broke Susanna's heart, knowing that her own daughter had had a hand in her granddaughter's plight.

Jenna was at the pinnacle of her fame and had achieved utter perfection on the violin. It was no wonder that her granddaughter was so proficient. Jenna gave all that she had to the instrument that, in Susanna's opinion, couldn't give anything back. Inanimate objects couldn't take the place of flesh and bone, muscle and strength, heat and fire.

And Jenna had never experienced fire.

Susanna studied her granddaughter's clothing, dressed as she was in a pair of tailored gray pants, pink silk blouse and a classic gray blazer. She was the epitome of the sophisticated prima performer, yet there was a core of steel in this young woman, a formidable will and a heart of gold.

Before she went, Susanna was determined that she would give her granddaughter a chance at love.

"There is something I must tell you." The weariness was dragging her down and she knew there wasn't enough time to tell Jenna everything.

"What is it?" Jenna said in alarm.

"Time is running out and I'll not be with you much longer."

"I know that, Gran." The pain and sadness in Jenna's voice pulled at Susanna's heart. Susanna's life was over, and she would never leave the hospital, but Jenna still had time, time to change.

"Do you?" She lifted the book from its resting place against her breast. "This is the last of my two diaries. The other one is in the desk."

"What desk?"

"Jenna, get the missing diary and protect them both. I was wicked—parties, men, scandal. Now those diaries could hurt them."

"Who, Gran?"

"There's sensuous jewelry." She grabbed Jenna's arm. "Keep all of it safe. Those men have families, important lives. Please, the diaries...the jewelry..."

Susanna closed her eyes, felt her strength slipping away. She squeezed her granddaughter's hand for the last time. "Promise me!"

"I promise."

"Come closer, child," Susanna said. Jenna's face swam before her eyes. When Jenna complied, Susanna pressed the delicate gold heart and fine chain into her hand. "Cherish this locket..."

"Gran."

"Find the diaries. Protect them. Read them."

Jenna was speaking to her, but the warm hand on Susanna's face distracted her. When she turned her head, her husband was there. With a deep sigh, she let go. Jenna would have to learn on her own that there was more to life than music.

As she slipped further away from the corporeal world, her final thought was for Jenna. There had been no contest between her husband and her music. She'd chosen the man she loved more than life. Her own daughter had chosen music and paid the price in heartbreak.

As she flew on the wings of happiness to her final destination, with her husband's hand clasped in hers, Susanna hoped it wasn't too late for her granddaughter to change the decision she'd made.

1

"JENNA! I NEED TO SPEAK to you! Open the door! Jenna!'' The banging on the front door distracted her from her thoughts. She knew that voice. It was her agent and friend Sarah McAllister.

Jenna got to the door, undid the new locks and let Sarah in.

Sarah stormed past Jenna and started jerking off her coat. "I take a two-week vacation and when I get back, my secretary tells me that you want to cancel a tour that has taken me months to arrange, all for a charity event in some small town in Texas. Have you lost your mind? My name is going to be mud in this industry."

Jenna calmly took Sarah's coat and hung it in the hall closet. "Sarah, take a deep breath. I'm not ditching the tour. Your secretary got it wrong. I just need some time."

"How much time?" Sarah looked at her more closely and must have seen her grief and her worry. "What happened?"

"My grandmother died."

"Oh, my God. That'll teach me to go to a secluded island getaway. And you let me rant and rave. Why

didn't you stop me from making a fool of myself?''
Instantly contrite, Sarah took hold of Jenna's hands.

It was hard to believe that the woman who had
raised her from infancy was gone. Jenna's gran truly
was the only mother she had ever known. After
Jenna's birth, her mother had been eager to get back
to the glittering world of opera and couldn't be bothered with an infant. Meanwhile, Jenna's father was
too obsessed with his wife to be away from her for
any length of time. So both of her parents had drifted
from her, while her gran had taken on more and more
of the responsibility.

Jenna sat on her grandmother's camelback antique
sofa in the small parlor and Sarah followed.

Jenna's voice broke the stillness. ''I'd sit for hours
like this, drinking tea from a fine china cup and reading while Gran produced intricate lace doilies from
silken white thread. I can almost smell the cinnamon
cookies we were both fond of.'' The memory caused
her breath to jam in her chest. Unable to sit any
longer, Jenna got up and walked to the piano. She ran
her hand along the polished black cover that protected
the ivory keys. On the piano was one of those elaborate doilies, and numerous photographs in gleaming
gold frames. A visual catalog of her gran's life flashed
before Jenna's eyes.

''I remember how she used to sing her chords every
day, running up and down the scale with her magnificent voice. Her voice was very beautiful. It's easy to
understand why she was so popular.''

Sarah got up and walked over to the piano. She put
her hand on Jenna's shoulder and the light touch

seemed to give Jenna comfort. "Next to you, Jenna, your gran was the most amazing woman I've ever known. But you're stalling. Why the new door locks?"

Restless, Jenna rose and walked to the window. She stared out at the huge oak painted with the gentle hues of the fading sun.

"What's going on? Has something happened?"

"Sticky situation."

"So this jaunt to Texas has more to do with this *sticky situation* than it has to do with the fund-raiser for that hospital?"

Jenna nodded her head. "I couldn't face the house after the funeral—going through her things. It was too much."

"That's understandable, but why change the locks?" Sarah persisted.

"When I finally got over here, a week or so after the funeral, my uncle Paul was here cleaning out the place." Tears filled her eyes. "He'd been arranging it since before my gran's death and had my mother's help in getting into the house."

"That's terrible. It must have been hard for you to accept. What a despicable man—and your mother? I would have thought better of her. What did he do with your gran's beautiful belongings?"

"Sold them."

"But what does selling your gran's stuff have to do with the sticky situation?"

Tipping her head against the wall, Jenna stared harder at the oak and the slashes of color against its bark. "Before Gran died she told me that, well, that she'd been pretty wild in her younger days. During that time, she kept some diaries and chronicled her search for the perfect physical passion. She gave one of the diaries to me. The other one is in the desk.''

"Go, Susanna."

Jenna smiled faintly. "I was shocked, to say the least. I tried to get more details, but she was a bit incoherent and said the diaries were in the desk.

"She must have had at least three desks in her attic, in addition to some very pricey antiques. He sent all of it to an auction house and everything was sold."

Sarah looked aghast. "Oh. Now I see. The diary?"

Jenna walked over from the window. "I had Steven Miller, our lawyer, call the party who'd purchased the first of the three desks. The gentleman was quite gracious and allowed me to buy the desk back with ten percent added to the price he paid for it. I searched the desk when it arrived, but there was nothing in it."

Sarah looked puzzled. "So Mr. Miller called about the second desk?"

Jenna sat down. "Yes. This time it was a judge. But he wouldn't sell the desk back."

A look of unease flickered across Sarah's face. Jenna understood Sarah's anxiety. Whatever touched Susanna also affected Jenna. Sarah was aware of the unwanted publicity the diary would stir up. But Jenna wasn't worried about her own reputation. "Didn't Mr. Miller tell him that there were mementos hidden in the desk that belonged to your gran?"

"He did and it spelled disaster."

Sarah grimaced. "The judge said that anything in the desk belonged to him?" Sarah guessed. At

Jenna's nod, Sarah continued, "So was the diary in the desk?"

"No." Sarah's expression relaxed. "He allowed Mr. Miller to be present when he searched the desk, especially after Mr. Miller told him that the desk, though purchased legitimately, had been fraudulently acquired by my disreputable uncle."

"Which brings us to the third and final desk." Sarah clasped Jenna's hand. "It's in Texas?"

"A man by the name of Sam Winchester from Savannah, Texas, purchased the rolltop desk."

Sarah closed her eyes briefly, whether in dread or in relief, Jenna couldn't tell. "So that's why you're going there. You're going to search the desk yourself, aren't you?"

"I have to, Sarah. I can't take the chance that Mr. Winchester will act like the judge and lay claim to any articles hidden in the desk. He needs money to modernize Savannah's memorial hospital. Charity concerts would be a good way to raise money and a good excuse to get into his house."

Outside the living room, the sunset blazed and faded and Sarah stared at Jenna. Deep reservations about this hasty decision gleamed in Sarah's eyes. Sarah was paid and paid well to anticipate and ward off anything that would cause negative attention for her client, but Jenna cared more about her promise to her gran.

"You think people would be interested in a bunch of diaries written by a girl?" Sarah asked.

"Probably not some ordinary girl. But my gran wasn't ordinary. She was a phenomenon, a diva of the opera and she had affairs with men who are now very prominent citizens. She begged me to protect them and their families. It would be terribly damaging and scandalous to them.'' Jenna debated telling Sarah more bad news, but decided it would make her understand why it was imperative that Jenna go to Texas. ''And there's some very old and very valuable erotic jewelry hidden in the desk, too.''

At her words, she could see that Sarah was resigned to Jenna going to Texas. ''Jeez, this just keeps getting better and better. What kind of jewelry?''

''Jewel-encrusted nipple rings, a waist chain, and a jade necklace carved in a very distinct way.''

''Phallic?'' Sarah asked, her shoulders slumping in defeat.

''Oh yeah.''

''How did you find out about this charity event and how are you going to get into his house?''

That's what Jenna liked about Sarah. When she committed herself, she went forward without restraint. Jenna said, ''I hired a private investigator. He came up with all the details and gave me a cover. The story about the hospital's renovation is in *Entrepreneur Magazine,* and there's an interview with Mr. Winchester.''

''A cover?'' Uncertainty crept into her expression. ''Like a spy.''

''I'm not exactly spying. I just want the diary and the jewelry.''

''So you concocted what kind of story?''

''Actually, I need you to contact Sam for me and tell him that I would like to do two concerts and a workshop at their local college in exchange for an opportunity to experience a real, working Texas ranch.''

"How could the guy turn you down, since you're doing all this for free, right?"

"My thoughts exactly. Besides he's the chairman of the fund-raising effort. Who else would have me as a houseguest? It would only be for two weeks."

"Good point. How big is this town?"

"Midsize, but close to Houston and Galveston."

Jenna saw the gleam in Sarah's eye. "I can work with that. At least I can get some good publicity out of this fiasco."

"So you'll do it?" Jenna asked.

"You'll finish out the tour?"

Jenna felt some of the tension go out of her spine. "Cross my heart. Have I ever let you down, Sarah?"

October 8, 1957

It's now been six months since I started my journey of sexual awakening and I'm no closer to my goal. I've had experiences that have been carnally satisfying, fulfilling the needs of the body, but it doesn't seem to be enough. It's vaguely disappointing and I can't understand why. This is what I wanted, what I planned for, yet it hasn't given me as much pleasure as I expected. Perhaps I just haven't met the right man. I'll find that one perfect physical encounter. I just have to keep looking.

Jenna closed the diary and looked out the window of the 747 into the bright cloudless sky. It had always been Jenna's impression that Gran loved Gramps with all her heart. After reading this passage, she wondered why Gran had so desperately wanted her to read these diaries. She rather liked the love story she'd heard about her grandparents and didn't want to read about the other men in her gran's life.

The "fasten seat belt" light came on and the pilot announced their approach to the Houston airport, stating the time was one o'clock and that the weather on this fine April day was a mild seventy-three degrees.

Jenna reached down and reverently picked up the worn black violin case and opened the lid. Inside sat her instrument, a gleaming Stradivarius that had been a present from Gran and Gramps when she'd graduated from Julliard.

The thought of Julliard brought back many memories. Memories of how she'd left Rosewood, Connecticut, which had been Gran's respite from New York City. To Jenna, though, the Victorian house with the gazebo-like porch and the pointed roofs with the contrasting white gables was her home. The expensive apartment Gran had purchased for her, so that Jenna wouldn't have to commute during her four years at Julliard, didn't mean much to Jenna.

Julliard had been a bane and a boon. Because of her mother and grandmother's fame, Jenna was goggled at, given a wide berth, and, because of it, felt isolated and alone. She'd had nothing but the music to bolster her and she'd retreated into it, excelling at her studies, but only engendering more awe.

She hadn't wanted the awe. What she'd wanted was to belong, to be treated like everyone else.

She'd even tried singing, but that, too, made the students envy her, shun her or ignore her. Jenna was cursed with talent and it was just one more lesson in the many lessons she'd learned the hard way. Her music never shunned her, deserted her or asked for what Jenna couldn't give.

Even her gran had been somewhat insensitive to Jenna's needs. To her disappointment, Jenna had taken up the violin instead of developing her exceptional singing voice. Truth be told, Jenna didn't really want to go into a profession that would have her competing directly with her mother.

Jenna stroked the instrument with a soft cloth she kept in the case. Unable to help herself, she ran her hands over the strings. Just thinking about the sound of the sweet, pure notes it produced made her smile.

She closed the case and kept the violin in her lap. Grabbing her briefcase from under the seat in front of her, she tucked the diary inside.

Antsy and agitated at the reason for her impromptu journey, she gripped the seat arms as the plane touched down.

As she made her way to the gate, she vowed she wasn't leaving Savannah, Texas, until she got what she came for.

True to her promise, Sarah had participated fully in the scheme and sent Jenna's photo to Sam Winchester so he could recognize her at the airport.

Unfortunately, Jenna had no idea what Sam looked like. It was no matter; he was probably some aging, retired lawman with a potbelly and gray hair, who couldn't stop reliving stories of his thrilling time in the Rangers. She was pretty confident that she'd be able to wrap this old guy around her little finger.

A man caught her eye. In fact, he caught more than one eye. He was standing against the far wall, obviously waiting for someone, probably a sweetheart, since his fist was full of roses. One black-booted foot was propped against the wall, while the other long leg was braced to hold him upright. The brim of the black Stetson he wore obscured most of his face except for a strong jawline. His eyes were lowered to a piece of paper in his free hand.

He was wearing a black Western-style shirt, edged in white piping and, over the shirt, a beautiful black buckskin-fringed jacket with soft leather appliqué that featured white buffalo galloping around the hem of the short waist. The jacket covered a pretty impressive set of shoulders and a wide chest. A pair of tight, formfitting black jeans outlined sleek, heavy muscles molded to those long legs.

That was some lucky lady he was waiting for. For a moment, just a moment, Jenna felt envy that she wouldn't have a man like this waiting at JFK for her when she returned home.

The flight was announced again and the man's head jerked up as if he'd been studying the paper so hard he hadn't heard the flight information the first time. Jenna's lungs seized. He had an arresting face, a face that made several women behind her sigh in appreciation. Dark hair had escaped the hat and lay across his wide forehead above dark brows. His gaze collided with hers—his eyes were a clear, heartbreakingly deep blue, made all the more intense by his tanned face and the black hat he wore.

His surprised look had a glint of wariness, which put her a little on her guard. But then he smiled and pushed off the wall. His smile slammed into her with rock-hard force—it was filled with sin and danger.

He walked straight toward her with the cocky swagger of a man who looked as though he enjoyed living on the edge. Jenna couldn't take her eyes off him to see who the lucky woman was that had this cowboy focused with such intensity. When he stopped in front of her, it took Jenna a moment to realize she needed to step aside. But then she saw the picture in his hand. He thrust the flowers out to her and said, "Welcome to Texas, Miss Sinclair. It's nice to have you visiting. We appreciate all your help."

His voice was deep and resonated inside her like a pure, sweet sound—almost too beautiful to be true. For a moment, she couldn't speak as she hastily took the flowers he offered, juggling her briefcase and violin case. Her heart lurched into her throat and her pulse skipped a beat. Surely this must be some ranch hand that Sam Winchester had sent to pick her up. Perhaps he was busy, or sick.

"Mr. Winchester couldn't make it?"

"I'm Sam Winchester, but since we'll be living together, you can call me Sam." He offered his hand and Jenna awkwardly transferred the flowers into the crook of her left arm. She slid her palm over his work-roughened hand, the abrasion of his skin making her insides jolt and spin. His skin was warm, sending prickles of electric sensation up her arm to hum through her blood. She let go hastily.

"You're Sam Winchester?"

He removed the Stetson and twirled it in his hands, giving her a cute aw-shucks look. "Sure am. Who were you expecting?"

His hair was midnight-black, short on the top but longer in the back, curling around the collar of the jacket. "You, but you're not exactly what I imagined."

His voice was teasing and easy as he drawled, "A dusty cowboy with hay in his hair?"

"No. An aging sheriff with a big gut."

He laughed, flashing that oh-so-dangerous smile. "Sorry to disappoint you, ma'am."

"Who said I was disappointed?" The comment came out of her mouth before she engaged her brain. He sent her another smile and tilted his head as if he wasn't quite sure about her.

Clearly, from the twinkle in his eye, flirting was fine with him. He put the hat back on his head. "We'd better pick up your bags and get going."

He reached for her briefcase and violin case, and Jenna recoiled from his touch.

"Pardon me."

"No. I'm sorry. Please, take the briefcase, but I am very protective of my instrument. I think I'll hold on to the flowers, too." She smiled, trying to alleviate the sudden tension between them.

"My apologies. I should have realized that musicians and their instruments are as inseparable as a cowboy and his horse."

He was far too charming, with his easy manner and his soft voice; she immediately relaxed and returned his smile.

At the luggage carousel, they waited side by side until her bags came whirling around. He plucked them off without any effort and indicated she should follow him.

"So why are you willing to come all the way to the wilds of Texas and perform for free?"

Jenna had already worked out an answer to this question. "I've been around the world to many glamorous places and have seen what every cosmopolitan city has to offer. So, when my agent told me about the article she'd read in *Entrepreneur Magazine,* about your effort to raise money to modernize the hospital, I couldn't resist. I think it's time I saw something of small-town life. Besides, yours is a good cause."

He nodded and they exited the airport. After a few minutes of navigating through parked cars, Sam stopped in front of a black-and-chrome truck. He set the bags down, and inserted a key in the passenger door lock. "So how did you know I was a lawman?"

Oops—that was in the report. She thought quickly. "I think someone at the college told me you used to be a Texas Ranger."

"I see." He opened her door for her, then placed her bags and briefcase into the back seat.

"Why did you stop being a lawman?" She set her violin on the floor just behind the seat and placed the roses on top of her suitcases. Then she eyed the truck. Because the vehicle sat quite a way off the ground,

Jenna had to lift her leg up and onto the running board. It wouldn't have been a problem if she'd worn a pair of slacks, but the pencil-thin black skirt didn't allow any leeway.

"My father got…ill and I came back to run the ranch. He died about a year ago," Sam answered, watching her with interest.

"Why did you leave the ranch in the first place?" she asked as if undaunted by the height and his obvious skepticism. She raised her leg, revealing a swath of thigh and immediately put her foot down. She tried different ways for a full minute, but she couldn't get up high enough to slide easily into her seat.

Amusement filled Sam's eyes as she struggled to figure out how to get in. "When I was eighteen, my father and I had a parting of the ways. I joined the Texas Highway Patrol right out of high school."

"I thought you were a Ranger." Jenna lifted her leg again, and again had to put it down.

"All Rangers are chosen from the ranks of the Texas Highway Patrol. So, once I did my eight years, I applied to the Texas Rangers, was accepted and served for two years, then I took over the ranch."

One moment she was standing in the Texas heat, trying to figure out how she was going to get into the truck and carrying on a conversation with him, and the next she was in his arms. The heat of his big body ran like electricity down her form from one end to the other.

"Is this considered truck-side service?" she asked, her eyes connecting with his.

She was very close to his face and for a moment he stared into her eyes. The mischief she had seen in them only moments ago intensified, deepened and co-alesced into something so intriguing she couldn't look away. Like a new piece of music when played, it gave such an exquisite sound that the listener had to pause, close one's eyes and savor the sound.

"As much as I enjoyed watching you try to ma-neuver into my truck in your tight, fancy skirt, I hadn't figured on spending the whole day here."

The thrilling sensation of his hands on her body and her breast against his hard pectoral muscle moved through her blood, and along her flesh in sharp waves. Right at that moment, lust, too deep and strong for her to deny, and more overwhelming than she'd ever experienced, made her want to lean in and taste his full mouth to see if it was as delicious as it looked.

He placed her in the cab of the truck, his hands lingering on her shoulder and thigh. When he slowly removed them, she wanted to reach out and capture his face in her hands and give in to the need swirling in her blood.

She settled in the seat as he came around the hood of the truck and climbed in. The space in the cab seemed to shrink with his presence.

She was here on a mission to retrieve the diary and jewelry, she reminded herself. With scepticism, she thought of her gran's words chronicled in the diary she'd read on the plane. Was there something that could be defined as perfect physical pleasure? Did she dare think that she could let herself go? No. It wouldn't be ethical to look for the diary while giving in to her baser needs. Would it? Trying to get back to some normalcy and defuse the suddenly tense atmosphere in the cab, Jenna murmured, "I'm sorry about your father, I just lost my gran."

He glanced at her, releasing a breath. Something tangible seemed to hover around them still. "I'm sorry, too. It's hard to lose someone you love. I didn't realize how much I missed the town and the ranch until my father died."

"We take a lot for granted, especially people we love and who love us. We don't realize how important they are, until we lose them." She looked out of the window at the magnificent skyline of Houston. "Do you miss being a Ranger?"

"Sometimes, but I love ranching. The place—the Wildcatter—has been in my family for generations. I couldn't sell it or trust anyone else to run it, so here I am."

The obvious pride in his voice was the same kind of pride that Jenna heard in her own voice when she talked about her music. "And your involvement with the modernization of the hospital? I find that intriguing."

"Every town needs a facility that can handle trauma emergencies and difficult medical situations. Although I had no idea that I was going to be dragged into policy matters and such."

"It sounds like you've gone above and beyond what any citizen would do."

"Well, I'm also the founding father's direct ancestor. In fact, the town is named after my great-grandmother, Savannah. The politicking that goes on keeps me knee-deep in cow…manure.''

''And you do that from the sidelines? You're not exactly the politician type.'' Too rugged, too out-doorsy—she had trouble imagining him in a suit sitting around a conference table discussing municipal problems.

He smiled and glanced at her. ''First, I'm not what you expected a former Ranger to look like. Now, Miss Sinclair, are you saying that I'm not smooth enough to be a politician?''

Unable to help herself, she smiled back. ''Please call me Jenna, and not exactly.'' She studied his face, couldn't stop her eyes from gazing at his body. He looked like he'd go down real smooth and have her begging for more. The words came out before she could stop them. ''You look too honest to me.''

Sam laughed and said, ''Ah, a burden I have to carry and one virtue the mayor agrees I have too much of.''

Right. He looked honest, but so had her uncle, a man who hadn't waited until her gran, his sister, was cold in the ground before he was trying to profit from her death. ''Something required in a lawman, but not necessarily valued in a public servant?'' She gave him a quick smile.

''So it would seem.''

''Part of the charm?''

The sparkle in his eyes turned into a wicked glitter. ''Aw shucks, ma'am.''

''Make that cowboy charm.''

He smiled. "I'd say that honesty in any relationship is important."

With a twinge, Jenna nodded her head. If only she could trust him. Sam didn't look like the kind of man who would cheat her out of her gran's mementos, but she couldn't take that chance.

"I'm looking forward to staying on your ranch."

He looked at her warily as they left the city and merged into highway traffic.

"What would you expect for your *ranch experience.*"

"Everything. I want to see what you do every day."

"You want to pay bills?"

"Well, maybe not that, but I want to get a feel for the cowboy life. I've always been fascinated with the Wild West concept," she improvised.

"My ranch is not like any TV show or movie if that's what you think. It's nice, but it's not glamorous."

Without thinking, she reached out and put her hand on his arm in a companionable gesture. "So no melodrama around the campfire?" Her mouth went dry at the feel of the corded muscles in his forearm and, for a moment, she couldn't remove her hand.

2

SAM WINCHESTER FELT heat swell inside him at the touch of her hand and the thought of this beautiful, sophisticated woman in his house. He wasn't a man to look a gift horse in the mouth. Yet he'd been down the city slicker path before with his ex-wife. Tiffany had been all excited to see his ranch, saying it would be a wonderful experience, but had then decided she couldn't stand it: the noise, the smelly cows, horses and, of course, him. She'd found many reasons to get off the ranch and away from him. Shopping sprees, trips to visit her upscale friends and snooty family, until there was nothing left between them but two gold rings and a lot of bitterness.

Jenna still hadn't removed her hand and it was beginning to distract him, along the lines of watching her try to find a ladylike way to get into his truck. "No, no melodrama. A lot of people think that ranching is romantic and exciting, but it's dirty, sweaty and hard work." This hothouse flower would probably take one look at the longhorns, pinch her nose and go running for the house. And she'd be dodging cow paddies in those out-of-place expensive heels along the way. The things on her feet were fine for Park

Avenue, but as useless, on a working ranch, as tits on a bull.

However, he couldn't think of anything wrong with the way she smelled. Her expensive, heady fragrance lodged in his brain, setting his senses on fire.

"I don't have any fancy expectations."

There was something about her answer that put his Ranger instincts on alert. Was it her tone that didn't ring true or the way her eyes slid away from his, as if she had something to hide? Suspects did that when they were lying.

He shrugged off his suspicions, realizing how silly they must be. He didn't believe that she wouldn't expect total pampering. He knew the type very well. Regardless, he didn't have the staff for that. Well, if she wanted the *ranch experience,* she could just take everything else that went with it. She'd be begging him to take her to a hotel within a day.

She was a fine little package all buttoned down and swept up. Shortly after he'd lifted her into the cab of the truck, she'd removed the black jacket that matched the narrow skirt she wore. Underneath the jacket, she revealed a tight white shirt that looked as soft as her skin. He'd almost driven off the road when he'd glanced at the blouse and seen the distinct outline of the lacy bra she wore beneath it, as if it offered him a peek at the forbidden.

Her shining coffee-colored hair, shot through with gold, was situated on top of her head in an elaborate, stylish twist. Her stark hairdo showed off the perfect, delicate features of her face. Wide, almond-shaped cinnamon-brown eyes, framed with dark brown lashes, hid treasures a man wanted to mine. Not with picks and shovels, but with hands, mouth and body until all her riches became his.

Sam turned down the dusty road that led to his ranch, and looked for her reaction, but she seemed enthralled with the countryside.

The sleek black truck topped the rise in the driveway. They passed through the wrought-iron arch with elaborate curlicues from which hung a sign that read The Wildcatter—Home of World-Class Cutters. She asked, "Why is your ranch named the Wildcatter?"

"My great-granddad, Silas Winchester, was a wildcatter." At her confused look, he sighed. "Men who search for oil are called wildcatters. Good ol' Silas struck it rich, sold his claim, came here and built this ranch."

When the ranch came into view, Sam pointed out a newly built arena. It was situated below an assortment of outbuildings and a big, elongated structure with corrals near a barn. Paddocks were visible in the distance—some filled with longhorns, others with horses. Beyond the arena was the big house. The foreman's cottage had been built in a beautiful wooded lot of pine and elm. The fencing showed off fresh paint, as did the barn. Everything gleamed.

Sam pulled up to the cedar-and-glass house and shut off the engine.

"This is a really modern outfit you have here."

Annoyance flashed through Sam. "Yes, ma'am, we update the buildings every hundred years or so, whether they need it or not."

She glanced at him, perhaps picking up the undertone of irritation in his voice, but he pretended not to notice and left the truck. He realized, as he walked around the vehicle, that he would also have to lift her out. That ridiculous skirt would force her to do a very unladylike slide off the seat to the ground and he guessed she wasn't even going to attempt that. Against his will, anticipation grew at the thought of touching her again.

He opened the passenger door and stood there for a moment as if waiting for permission to assist her. She reached behind her and snagged her violin case. "I would appreciate it if you could help me down."

Her prim and proper voice sent another shot of irritation through him. Honestly, he didn't have time to squire some city slicker gal around his ranch. But he had to remember this was for a good cause. "Yes, ma'am, we aim to please."

He slid his hand under her legs and he had to stifle a gasp at the heat of her skin through the nylon of her hose. He moved in closer and encircled her back with his other arm and, as easily as before, lifted her into his arms and started to walk. Her body was tight and hot against his. He wondered how her skin would feel. He wanted to get closer to have more than a tease of that compelling fragrance.

"Is this considered a neighborly gesture?"

"Huh?"

She smiled and he liked the way her dark brown eyes filled with light. "You carried me all the way to the porch. Did you think I might not be able to walk on my own?"

He suddenly realized that he had carried her to the

wraparound porch complete with rocking chairs. He'd gotten lost in her eyes, the feel of her body against him. A commotion at one of the corrals close to the house caught her attention and gave him a moment to gather his composure and set her down.

"What are those men doing?" She walked to the very edge of the porch and peered in the direction of the noise, shielding her eyes.

"Breaking a stallion. I raise championship roping horses, but they have to be broken to the saddle. That one in the corral was neglected and is half-wild. I've been contracted to train him."

"How exciting."

He shrugged. "Not my usual method of handling a stallion with that kind of innate ability. But sometimes, when they reach this age, a man on his back is all he understands."

"You're going to ride him into submission?"

"I'm going to have to."

"And you're skilled at this?"

"Ask me that when I get thrown and end up eating dirt. I need to join them as soon as I get you and your bags in the house." The devil gripped him and he thought that maybe this would be all it would take to get her off his ranch and into a hotel. His ex-wife had thought breaking a horse was exciting until she'd had to breathe the dust and sweat of a horse and man. "Why don't you watch? Part of the working-ranch experience."

Her chin lifted. "I'm a bit tired."

His eyes narrowed as he studied her face. "I'll be breaking other broncs while you're here."

"It's not that I'm not interested."

"I understand. Not all cowboy things are appealing." It was true. She had said she wanted the full package, but he was also convinced she wouldn't like half the things she saw.

"Are you saying that because I'm from the city? That I wouldn't be able to handle seeing a cowboy break a horse or be able to keep up with you?"

"If the glass shoe fits."

Her features tightened and she looked up at him. "Are you challenging me?"

He tilted his head, hooked his thumbs in his jeans and slid out his hip. "Sure am."

"Lead the way."

"Not in those clothes. Do you have something else?"

"I have a pair of black slacks."

"More serviceable shoes? Could I hope for boots?"

"No. I'm afraid not. Loafers."

"Didn't you think to pack more practical clothing?"

"Slacks and loafers are my practical clothing."

"I guess they would be. They'll have to do. Tomorrow you can buy some ranch duds in Savannah."

He showed her into the house.

He entered an octagon-shaped foyer with gleaming hardwood floors and stained clerestory windows on six sides of the circular ceiling. A chandelier, which reflected a glorious rainbow of light throughout the entrance, was breathtaking. A glass-and-crystal table with delicate legs sat on a gilt pedestal. Large creamy-white orchids graced the table in an exquisite array, the scent of the exotic flowers floating on the sun-drenched air.

She looked up into his face. "I thought you said ranching wasn't glamorous. This looks pretty glamorous to me."

"Remnants of the influence of my ex-wife, Tiffany."

"Oh. It's beautiful."

"That's Tiffany. She liked beautiful things." He took her elbow and the heat of her was like the feel of flame against skin as he guided her into the living room.

A young man came out of a swinging door, revealing a glimpse of a gleaming kitchen and an older rotund woman standing at a counter.

Sam said, "This is Cal. He's Red and Maria Sparks's son and she is my housekeeper. Cal does odd jobs for me and also helps his mother with jobs in the house."

"Hi, Cal. I'm pleased to meet you." She shook the boy's hand.

"Pleased to meet you, ma'am."

"Cal, could you get Miss Sinclair's bags? She'll be staying with us for a little while."

"Right away."

The boy disappeared out the front door and soon returned with her bags and briefcase as Sam headed toward an impressive wooden staircase.

He stopped on the second floor in front of a doorway, ushering Jenna inside. The room, decorated in a charming Southwestern style, had a four-poster bed, hand-painted dresser and an adjacent bathroom.

"As soon as you're dressed, come downstairs and we'll go out to the corral."

His hand lingered on her elbow and she turned to look up at him. Her eyes were such a beautiful enticing brown. Her chin raised, as if he expected her to try to get out of joining him.

"I would love to watch," she said, her tone firm.

He liked the heightened color in her face, her snapping eyes. With a deliberate smile, he tipped his hat and backed out of the room. Cal passed him and deposited the bags on the beautiful lounge near the bed. He handed her the roses.

"Thank you, Cal," she said in that proper voice.

"Could I get a vase for these flowers?" she asked.

He nodded and left the room, shutting the door behind him.

Sam smiled to himself as he returned downstairs. Once she had a whiff of sweaty horse and got her expensive duds all dirty, she'd hightail it into Savannah and out of his way.

He didn't like his reaction to her on a purely physical level and he was not the kind of man who refused sex or the attentions of a beautiful woman. But Jenna was in a different league and he'd ridden that horse and been thrown. It was a good thing that she was going to be here for only a couple of weeks. The chemistry between them was irresistible. He could envision himself between her creamy thighs, his mouth moving over her body, taking what he wanted. Perhaps sheathing himself into her luscious body would take the edge off his libido.

But his Ranger instincts told him that he'd better slow that horse down.

WHEN SAM WALKED UP to the corral fifteen minutes later, his foreman, Tooter Dobson, stood at the fence and eyed him as he approached. The old man was dusty, his face streaked with dirt. His eyes shifted to Jenna and his brows rose as he took in her attire, his gaze stopped at her sleek upswept hairdo.

"Howdy, boss. Is this the fiddler?"

Sam could almost hear the censure in his simple words. *Another city slicker, Sam. Are you plumb crazy?* Tooter should know by now that Sam wasn't crazy enough to take up with Jenna for anything as serious as a real relationship.

"Tooter Dobson, my foreman."

"Nice to meet you."

Sam situated Jenna at the fence so she could see. The other hands eyed one another and he knew they were all thinking that their boss shouldn't ever get involved with a fancy piece again.

When Tooter didn't move, Sam ducked under the fence and said, "Are we going to stand here all day, or break that stallion to the saddle." Sam threw black chaps over the split-rail fence.

Tooter turned, barely hiding his grin. "Breaking a horse is not usually your way, Sam." He pulled the worn, much abused hat off his head and sent his hand through a curly mass of sandy hair. "I know you like to sweet-talk 'em, but I have to tell you, he's about the orneriest, most stubborn horse I've come into contact with." He paused for a moment, eyeing the horse as he pranced around the arena while three ranch hands tried to corner and catch him. "He don't like the saddle or the weight of a man on his back."

Jenna gripped the rough wood of the fence beneath her hands. Despite the fact that she'd wanted to use this moment as an opportunity to search for the diary, Jenna was intrigued. Sam watched as the ranch hands finally succeeded in catching the elusive animal. They led the seemingly complacent horse back over to Tooter. Sam snagged the chaps off the fence. He fit them to his waist and slipped the buckle into place. He tightened the belt on the chaps, which clung to his hips like a second skin. Oh my, could the man get any sexier? Pulling the gloves free from his waistband, he said, "Then let's try it the hard way."

"Sam, don't be too cocky. He's a tough feller," Tooter warned.

"I'm not cocky, just more stubborn than he is. Sometimes teaching humility hurts."

Tooter laughed. "Darn right. What I want to know is who's doing the teaching and who's doing the learning?"

"That remains to be seen," Sam said to Tooter. Sam smiled and turned to Jenna. "Red Sparks and Frank Howard," Sam said, introducing the other two hands who had been standing at the fence watching their boss. Jenna nodded to each and they both smiled and tipped their hats.

Red crowed with delight. "Ride 'em, boss! Show that bucking bronc who's in charge."

The horse tried to bite Sam and Sam pushed his head away. "Stop fighting so hard, buddy. I'm not going to hurt you. Once you realize that, we can get down to roping. That's what you like, isn't it?"

The horse snorted and tossed his head, sidling nervously away from the familiar voice as if to say, *Don't try it or you'll be sorry.* Something tightened inside of Jenna and her chest started to hurt.

She should be looking for the diary, but when he'd challenged her, she couldn't help rising to the occasion. She'd bite her tongue before she told him that she hadn't thought about packing ranch *duds* because she hadn't been much interested in the ranch at all. She wasn't here to find her inner cowgirl. She was here for her grandmother.

One of the ranch hands covered the horse's eyes with a bandanna and Sam bent down, grabbed the leather strap across the horse's belly and took up the slack. The horse snorted and stamped, but he allowed Sam to tighten the strap. Sam put his foot in the stirrup and Jenna's heartbeat soared as she watched the horse quiver.

Jenna couldn't take her eyes away from Sam as he mounted and tucked his other foot in the empty stirrup. He sat deep in the saddle and lifted one arm. Wrapping his other hand in the reins, he took a firm hold with his legs. His eyes met those of the man responsible for removing the blindfold. Sam nodded to him and he pulled the material away.

The result was immediate, spectacular and terrifying. With a squeal of defiance, the stallion performed a straight-in-the-air hop, but Sam was ready for him and the jarring landing didn't unseat him. He tightened his legs and his body moved with the bucking motion of the stallion.

"Oh my God."

"He's a pistol, our Sam." Tooter's eyes gleamed with pride as he watched Sam.

"I've never seen anything like it," Jenna admitted. "Is he this focused in everything he does?"

Tooter looked at her, then said, "Yep. Whether it be calving, roping, riding or branding. Sam's focused in everything he does."

"And here I thought he was a charming, pampered cattle baron."

Tooter snorted. "Don't get me wrong, little lady. Sam likes his creature comforts right enough, but he's not afraid to get his hands dirty."

Eight seconds passed, ten, twenty and finally, with a powerful kick of the stallion's hindquarters, Sam was thrown. He hit the ground hard, obviously trying to catch his breath. One man helped him up while the other patted his back.

"Teach him a lesson yet, son?" Tooter called.

Sam grinned right through the grime and sweat.

"Or did he teach you?" Red asked.

Sam laughed. With that full smile on his face, Sam's eyes riveted to Jenna's and her breath caught. A blue flame was all she could compare his gaze to, and Jenna hadn't ever experienced fire like that.

As soon as the stallion was caught, Sam pulled his gaze from hers and was on his back again.

Jenna cringed each time Sam was unseated and ended up in the dirt, her stomach fluttering at the stupid feelings trapped inside—excitement, fear and awe. They all rolled around inside her as the afternoon wore on. Jenna watched as Sam was thrown so many times that she lost count.

But each time he got back on the horse, those big hands wrapped around the reins. Staring at his hands made her remember the way they had slipped under her knees, the easy way he'd picked her up and held her to his strong chest. She couldn't get it out of her mind.

When Sam was thrown again, Jenna winced.

Her breath caught in her throat. Gone was the easy way about him, gone was the mischievous twinkle, and gone was the teasing. This man, this gutsy, strong man, had replaced that man.

And he was sexy.

Oh, so sexy.

Man and animal sparred. The look on Sam's face was firm and tough. His hat was jammed on his head, pulled low over his intense eyes like an outlaw. There was tensile strength in him—in the tough curve of his clenched jaw, in the depth of his alert eyes, in the rock-hard line of his body.

A shiver of apprehension sailed through her. If he was this tenacious with the stallion, she could only guess how he'd be in bed. She tried to ignore it—the rhythm of his big body, the valiant efforts of the strong animal beneath him—but she couldn't seem to stop thinking about how he would make love to her.

Suddenly, without any warning, the wildly bucking horse tilted into the fence right near her and she jumped back as hundreds of pounds of enraged horseflesh made the fence vibrate under her grip. She heard Sam grunt in pain and caught a whirl of blue eyes and a grimy face before the horse danced away.

It was in that moment that she realized how much control, tenacity and sheer guts it took for a man to climb up on such a huge beast and attempt to tame him.

The tired animal was beginning to show the strain as he stumbled and caught himself. He slowed, trotted for a few feet, bucked once more, then he evened out. It was over, but it was clear to Jenna, as Sam bent down to rub at the horse's damp neck, that it had been a battle of wills and no one had really won. It had been a contest to see who could endure. Sam showed his respect by taking the saddle and bridle off the animal himself, and Jenna watched as he slipped the halter over the horse's head. He took up the lead rope and led the sweat-soaked horse slowly around the ring to cool him down.

She smiled as he took a nip at Sam's arm.

Jenna waited until Sam led the stallion from the corral. Sam watched her intently.

"I'm sure you'd like to go up to the porch. I'll call from the barn and have Mrs. Sparks bring you some lemonade."

"Aren't you coming?"

Sam's head came up and her eyes collided with his. "No. I've got a messy job to do. You wouldn't want to ruin your expensive shoes," he said softly. He turned away and started to lead the horse around in circles.

"Well, what did you think of that, little lady?"

Jenna turned to find Tooter at her arm. "It was quite exciting," she said, unable to stop her eyes from roaming to Sam. "They were both pretty determined."

"Sam has that in abundance, along with a lot of pride." A bell rang in the distance. "That's grub. Gotta go or the ravenous young'uns will have eaten everything." He tipped his hat and sauntered off.

When she turned to seek out Sam, he was gone. She went into the barn to find him, her blood pumped with adrenaline. He'd cross-tied the horse and was using the hose to get the worst of the grime off the animal. Jenna stopped and swallowed hard. Sam was bare from the waist up. He was still clothed in his tight jeans and the sexy black shotgun chaps. The Stetson was still on his head and shielded his eyes from her.

Unable to think of the right thing to say to him, but unable to leave, she blurted out, "Sam, are you hurt?" Not the most sophisticated way to act, but he made her feel on the edge of a cliff.

His head jerked up and he stared at her.

"I heard you make a noise when he slammed into the fence."

"Just a passel of bruises. Nothing serious." He shrugged, seeming out of sorts to her. "Go on up to the house."

It irked her that he didn't think she belonged here. She might be from New York, but she wasn't averse to horses or barns. She definitely was not averse to him. Not with all that hard-wrought muscle evident in his thick biceps. "Can't I help?"

He looked over at her and shook his head. Walking around the horse, he picked up a pair of black rubber boots. "Here, slip these on," he said without inflection.

Jenna slipped on the oversize boots. Sam grabbed a bucket and began to pour in warm water, adding equine soap and a bit of mineral oil. He held out a sponge.

She dropped the sponge into the bucket and rolled up her sleeves. She'd show him she wasn't afraid of hard work. She'd washed her own car plenty of times. It couldn't be too hard and she didn't have to put on a coat of wax.

She grabbed the soapy sponge and began to wash one side of the horse. She knew the moment Sam stepped behind her. She could feel his chest close to her back; she could feel the heat of his body. "Jenna, this way," he said in a husky voice. "Follow the way his hair grows."

His big hand engulfed hers and Jenna had to close her eyes at the sensations that zinged through her from his callused touch. Working man's hands, abrasive and warm, competent and kind.

"You usually do these chores yourself?"

He didn't remove his hand, not even when she started to wash the horse correctly.

"Not usually. Cowboys don't really spend a whole lot of time grooming their horses. But this one isn't mine. I need to take extra care. The business side of the ranch takes up most of my day, but this is what ranching is all about." She sucked in a breath when he moved closer to her, the feel of his mouth soft and hot against the shell of her ear.

"See, he likes that." The cadence of his voice was intoxicating as she unconsciously leaned back. Turning her head, the side of his face came into view. That steel jaw, the dark stubble, and his perfect, tantalizing ear with the fleshy lobe.

Something in the barn fell to the floor and the clatter drew them apart. Sam cleared his throat. "Let's get to the other side." He picked up another sponge and started to wash the horse's hindquarters.

When they had finished, Jenna stepped back as Sam picked up the hose. He rinsed while Jenna smiled at the way the animal tried to catch water in his mouth by tossing his head. "I think he must be thirsty."

"Looks like it. Would you grab a clean bucket and get him a drink?" Sam asked.

Jenna did so. When she came back with the bucket, the eager horse sidestepped the stream of water directed at him and the spray hit her right in the face.

She squealed from the sudden attack and the cold feel of the water.

"Damn. I'm so...sorry," he said.

She placed the bucket down so that the thirsty horse could drink. "You did that on purpose." Jenna then picked up the bucket filled with dirty water.

"I swear I didn't." Sam eyed the bucket in her hands. "You wouldn't dare," he challenged.

"Oh, yes, I would," she refuted with narrowed eyes that twinkled with merriment.

He grinned and Jenna found it infectious.

"Don't do it, sugar pie," he warned, "or you'll be sorry."

"Oh, I will, will I?" she challenged him right back.

Sam used the hose on her again. Jenna tossed the contents of the bucket at him and launched herself toward him, trying to wrestle him for the hose. Their laughter mingled and, before Jenna knew what was happening, he had her pressed against his chest, her soft curves yielding to the hard contours of his body, a beautiful grin on his lips and an unsettling awareness in his eyes.

Prudently, she stepped back and he made a hissing sound as his eyes became riveted to the bodice of the white blouse.

She looked down to find that the water had soaked the silk and her lacy white bra, revealing the dusky disks of her nipples. Immediately, they puckered as she thought of Sam's eyes on her and all the adrenaline surged back into her body.

"Sam, you still in here?" The sound of Tooter's voice sent Sam into action. The next thing she knew, he was draping his coat around her shoulders. She pushed her arms through the sleeves and closed the coat over her breasts. The coat was a mess and smelled like a horse, but it was the sweetest gesture any man had ever made to her.

"Why don't you go on up to the house and shower and change. Mrs. Sparks probably has dinner ready about now. I'll see you there."

Jenna left the barn with one last, lingering look at all the hard muscle of his torso. Sam Winchester sure wasn't what she'd expected and she was just beginning to wish he *had* been some old, potbelly guy.

3

RAIN DRIPPED off the slightly too big hat that was perched on her head as she followed closely on Sam's heels.

The next morning, overcast and ugly, proved that maybe her plan wasn't such a hot idea as Sam, who seemed impervious to the rain, held the barn door open for her. She slipped inside and was assailed with the smell of warm horseflesh, fresh hay and an earthy scent she rather liked.

It reminded her of the spring, when tulips would push up from the dark earth and bloom along with flowering azaleas and Gran's well-tended rosebushes. Jenna could remember the days when she'd sit and watch her gran prune the bushes with a stylish floppy straw hat on her head. Elegant even as she toiled in the garden.

With the smell came the sharp sense of loss and Jenna closed her eyes.

"Hey, do you need another cup of coffee?"

She opened her eyes to find a chipper Sam, his eyes filled with mischief and a grin on his face. It had been six o'clock when he'd knocked on her door and told her to get up and get dressed. The *full ranch experience* was even better before the crack of dawn. What this smart-alecky cowboy wasn't aware of was that she always got up at six o'clock in the morning to practice an hour before breakfast. It limbered her up for the day.

"No. The smell in here reminds me of spring days when I used to watch my gran work in the garden."

"Oh, I'm sorry. I find myself doing that, too. I'll see a bridle hanging on a hook and I'll remember my dad's hands as he put the bridle on a horse. Strange what you remember, huh?"

"Yes, it is."

He handed her a scoop. "You can give them all one ration of grain. I'll fill the buckets."

"Yes, sir."

"You asked for it."

"I guess I did." She tipped her head back, gasping as the rain on the brim of her hat went down the back of her shirt. She removed the overly large hat. "I won't be running to a hotel, if that's what you think." She had a mission and, no matter how uncomfortable he made her, she wasn't leaving without Gran's belongings.

He gave her an innocent-as-a-babe look. "Why would I think that?" he asked, walking over to one of the stalls and tipping the bucket so that the water splashed into the trough.

"Oh, could it be that you dragged me out of bed early enough that it was still dark out, brought me into this downpour and now have me filling buckets with grain?"

"This trickle barely counts as a gully washer. Besides, downpours are good. Good for the grass and the streams. Sprinkles are for tenderfeet. Don't want to be a tenderfoot, do ya?''

She smiled. He was irresistible. Even when the man was being downright sneaky, he was too cute for words. ''Oh, good God, no. I wouldn't want to be labeled a tenderfoot. Perish the thought.''

He grinned at her. In his duster and Stetson, he looked like a poster boy for the rugged cowboy. She watched as he removed the coat and grabbed two baling hooks. He stuck the hooks into a bale of hay and dragged it over to the stalls. Dropping it at her feet, he replaced the baling hooks, picked up a pitchfork and began to fork hay into the first stall.

Jenna watched him, watched the sheer quality of movement, nothing wasted. She'd seen better-polished men, more well-spoken, but nothing fascinated her like watching Sam do manual labor.

''So why don't you want me here?''

She picked up a pitchfork herself. Sam paused and took notice of her for a moment. Then he shook his head and continued working.

''I didn't say I didn't want you here.''

''You didn't have to. It's only for a couple weeks.''

''I'm grateful to you, Jenna. I guess I just *like* dragging a city girl out of her warm bed to show her what real ranching is all about.''

''Would it surprise you that I get up at this time every morning?''

He stopped pitching hay and leaned his hands on top of the fork. ''That does surprise me.''

''I thought it would. I like practicing first thing in the morning.''

He looked sheepish. "And I dragged you out here in the rain, interfering with your schedule."

"I don't mind, really."

He stared at her a moment.

"Okay, it's wet and it's miserable," she admitted.

He nodded and bent to the hay again. "Let me know next time if I keep you from your practicing."

"I will."

HOURS LATER they finished the chores in that small part of the barn. Jenna rolled her shoulders, feeling tight, a bit of fatigue between her shoulder blades.

Sam saw her movement and concern crossed his features. The big, strong cowboy wanted her off his ranch, but he didn't want her hurt in the process. The thought gave a little tug on her heart.

He turned her gently and grasped the top of her shoulders. Using his fingers to massage her neck, his thumbs rubbed deeply and rhythmically around her shoulder blades.

Every muscle, every nerve in her body froze. Her heart stopped for an instant, then doubled its beat, the blood pushing rapidly through her veins to pound in her pulse.

His hands gentled, slowed until he was caressing instead of kneading. The silence in the barn thickened, stretched, teased and solidified into something completely different. Something alive. It smelled of leather and wood and hard work. It felt like the unraveling ties of restraint.

"Boss? You in here?"

Sam released her immediately and cleared his voice before he called out. "In here, Tooter."

Tooter came into the area where Jenna and Sam stood now a respectable distance apart. He tipped his hat. "Miss Sinclair."

"Please, Tooter, call me Jenna."

He nodded and turned to Sam. "Silver Shadow is getting ready to drop her foal and I'm worried about her. She's not actin' right."

"I'll be right there."

Tooter tipped his hat to her again, and said, "Ma'am," as he left the barn.

She looked up at Sam. "I see you're quite in demand here."

"That I am. If you'd like to go on up to the house and practice, I'll check out that pregnant mare."

"I don't mind."

"I've already interrupted your schedule enough," he said, and shrugged into his duster, pulling his hat low over his eyes. "You have that first concert tonight."

Jenna didn't argue. As much as she would like to see a foal born, he had reminded her that music was something much safer, something she understood more than this out-of-control feeling she got whenever he touched her.

She'd seen firsthand how hurt her father had been when her mother made opera the center of her world. Her brokenhearted father had never recovered and, to this day, Jenna had no idea where he was. Jenna never wanted to hurt anyone like that, especially a proud man like Sam. It was a promise she'd made to herself a long time ago, one she never intended to break.

Music was her life.

THAT NIGHT, Jenna stood in the wings and peeked out at the audience. Earlier, she'd wanted to locate the desk, but practicing and rehearsing with the Savannah College Orchestra didn't leave her any time.

Apprehension coursed through her, but it wasn't in response to all the people waiting for her to play her violin. She never got stage fright. No, this nervousness was a direct result of the fact that, against her own will, she wanted Sam to like her music as much as she'd enjoyed their early-morning chores.

In addition to her other selections, she'd chosen to play a special arrangement called "Storm." It was a hauntingly beautiful piece. She hoped it would appeal to Sam. Then she snorted at the unexpected thought. The man had dragged her around in the pouring rain to feed horses and cows. Why would she think he'd care about her music and why did it matter so much?

"A full house tonight, Miss Sinclair," the stage manager of the sumptuous Savannah College Tannenbaum Auditorium said to her with a pat on her shoulder. She smiled at him. He returned her smile.

"I heard you warming up. Your fiddling sounds mighty fine."

"Thank you. You're very kind."

"It's not kindness, if you'll pardon me for saying so, but admiration and the doggone truth."

"Thank you, then, for your admiration." She liked his nice plain face and charming Texas voice.

Not like Sam's. No, Sam's drawl was husky and seemed to seep into her bones.

She shook herself. The only reason she was even in Savannah was to get her gran's diary and jewelry back.

The hall continued to fill as people greeted each other and others searched for their seats. It was a handsome crowd, dressed in dark suits and fashionable gowns, some even aglitter, the light reflecting off numerous beads.

The house lights went down and the stage manager whispered, "Two minutes."

Jenna picked up her violin and fluffed up the flounces of her angle-length full-skirted black dress. Sam had been delayed in the foaling barn and she hadn't seen him before she left the ranch, driven to the college by one of his ranch hands.

She took a deep breath as she was announced. She swept out from the wing and walked to center stage. She refused to look at Sam, who was in the first row along with the mayor and his wife. Instead, she kept her eyes straightforward. She bowed into the applause. Then she brought her eyes to the seats directly in front of her and almost dropped her instrument.

She stared.

Her eyes met and melded with the piercing blue of his. They were hot eyes, eyes that promised heat beyond her wildest imagination. It was pure undiluted lust. There was not a man of her acquaintance who ever instilled this feeling inside her. In fact, every other man she had ever known paled in comparison to him.

In a sea of suits, Sam stood out in a black frock coat just like a riverboat gambler, with a striking silver-and-gray-tone vest over a white-banded collar shirt.

She remembered the determined look on his face yesterday afternoon when he'd broken the horse. She sensed strength in him, yet beneath his dress clothes there hid subtle danger. A whisper of risk.

He met her eyes boldly and, with an amused glint, he inclined his head slightly.

Her gaze moved down to his provocative mouth, wondering suddenly what it would be like to kiss such full, beautifully shaped lips.

His enticing mouth, turning up into a sweet smile, broke the spell and she pulled her eyes away. She said, "Good evening, ladies and gentlemen. It's a pleasure and an honor to be here tonight. I'm thrilled to be playing with the excellent Savannah College Orchestra and its illustrious conductor, Martin Slade." She extended her hand and the audience broke into applause.

She glanced back down at Sam, his presence commanding her attention. She raised her eyes to the conductor and nodded. He sharply rapped his baton at her commanding nod. Bringing the violin to her chin and the bow to the strings, she began to play. She moved from one piece to the next. The college orchestra was good, the music beautifully performed and the audience sighed collectively when they finished.

Sam hadn't been able to take his eyes off her from the moment she'd come onto the stage. When she spoke again into the microphone after several selections, her soft voice flowed over him. "I have looked forward to visiting Texas and I'd like to take this opportunity to thank Sam Winchester for being my gracious host." She looked down at him and smiled. "I would like to play for you a special work. I hope you like it. It's called 'Storm.'"

As soon as she stopped speaking, the lights went abruptly out, leaving the auditorium in total darkness. A slash of lightning brightened the large room, replicated by a strobe light. Then a hushed sound moved through the theater as thunder, skillfully played on the bass drums, could be heard very faintly in the distance.

She brought the gleaming violin to her chin once more. She drew the bow across the strings and a soft melodic note floated from the stage to captivate her audience. She held the note, let it waver and then drop softly into silence. When a flash of lightning filled the theater, followed by the soft grate of thunder, she repeated the deep melodic sound, holding it, and then moving her fingers in a sharp curve down to a deeper booming brassy note. Her fingers flew over the strings as Sam closed his eyes and let the music seduce him.

She played sharper notes in a staccato beat, the deep hollow sound giving him goose bumps. The music seemed to be heavy with moisture. The melody hinted of the rain-soaked grasslands, whispered of wind and mist and glistening shadow that hung over the Rio Grande. It murmured with pattering drops of rain that the audience strained to hear, like an elusive noise just out of earshot yet tantalizingly close.

The music affected him at an elemental level and touched him profoundly in a soul-wrenching way, beckoning and irresistible. Her eyes sought out Sam's in the semidarkness and as she met his sultry blue eyes, desire, quick and hot, infused him, charged him until his nerve endings were on fire with the need and the scintillating power. The very air was electric.

Sam felt the notes cut through him all the way to something inner and secret. He didn't know why, but they aroused him, stirred his blood. Then he realized his whole body was on fire. He was riveted to his seat and watched for her face as each lightning bolt struck. He couldn't have looked away if he'd wanted to. In that moment, when their eyes met, he knew he had to have her or go crazy with the wild savageness that was consuming him.

Gooseflesh rippled across his skin as if a breeze had suddenly blown through the auditorium. He wanted to leave his seat and touch her. Pull her against him, kiss her mouth, thrust into her with hard, demanding strokes, and make her completely his. It was as if he were caught in the silken web of an overpowering compulsion, as if she were the Pied Piper and he the beguiled mouse caught under her spell.

He breathed deeply to relieve some of the tension in his body. He realized he was sweating. Women didn't usually catch him off guard, but this compelling woman, with her bold eyes, had done just that. It felt as if the ground had been pulled away from him and had sent him spinning out of control.

Winsome, charming, bewitching...all those words

fit, but no language except the language of the gods could describe the sense of energy and vital essence, the force of spirit within Jenna's delicate features. Her face demanded attention and held it with a magnetic presence. But Sam knew, even if she'd been hidden in a crowd, he would have noticed her with her fine eyes and soft, upswept hair.

Lightning crackled, thunder rumbled, and with each illumination of her face and graceful body, he wanted her more and more until his blood was throbbing with it, beating in time to the delicate, haunting notes drawn from the instrument in her hands.

Sam felt power running though his bones, flesh, fingertips and shaft. She played the final note and waited for the last flash of lightning. The hushed admiration of the audience barely registered with Sam as another flash came. He left his seat and made his way backstage. Compelled by an unseen force that enticed him, drew him with uncontrollable desire. As she stepped into the wing, she collided with his solid form.

He curled steel-fingered hands around her upper arms, steadying her. He so startled her that she almost dropped her instrument.

"Jenna, I..." His voice came out husky and breathless.

Sam had never been so aware of a woman as he was of Jenna Sinclair. His body was tense and throbbing. Her sweet scent teased his senses. Even in the dimness he could discern the voluptuous curves of her body, thinking how perfectly she would fit to him.

"Sam...Sam, I need to change. I don't want to be

late for the reception.'' She peered up at him with wide brown eyes, almost making him reel at her closeness. Moments passed by. He took a deep breath to hang on to his resolve and to savor her delicious fragrance.

''Right. I came to drive you over to the hotel.''

''Thanks.''

He let go of her and followed her as she made her way to her dressing room. ''Would you like me to wait outside for you?''

''No, I need help with the zipper.''

He followed her inside and Jenna presented her back to him. He pulled down the zipper, his hands tingling at the feel of her silky back. She moved away from him, disappearing behind an ornate screen.

He could hear the rustle of her clothing as she took off the dress, and he closed his eyes and swallowed hard.

When she turned on a light behind the screen, he caught sight of her provocative silhouette and froze. Feeling as if something had thudded into his chest, he fixed his gaze on her, his pulse suddenly heavy. The white light and her dark outline made him think of white sheets and black velvet nights.

His breath jammed in his chest. He watched as she raised her hands over her head and something slinky cascaded down her graceful body, over peaked breasts to the tops of her shapely thighs. Enthralled, enticed, he moved toward the screen. Pressing his fingertip against the screen, he traced the curve of her breasts, the flare of her hips.

He closed his eyes against the surge of desire inside

him, and tried to regain control. She was a city slicker. She lived the same kind of life his ex-wife had left and then regretted once she found herself on an isolated ranch. But Jenna would be gone in a short period of time. He could let his desire reign free. There was danger in letting himself do so, in letting himself get close to her. Traveling, touring, fame were distinct parts of her life, a life she wouldn't give up. Wasn't that what he really wanted—no attachments? Now it made her especially appealing to him.

His hand was still on the screen when she emerged. She stared up at him with a startled look in her soft eyes. She looked at the screen, the light and the distinct outline of the clothing she'd discarded. Her eyes came back to his, sparks igniting in the sultry depths, and she made a helpless sound in her throat. The thought of her hot, silky skin and the sizzling look depleted his resolve. He swiftly captured her against him. The shimmering desire he'd been struggling with raged beyond his power to control, and reason faded.

She gasped as his rough mouth found hers. Softer than the finest velvet, her lips tasted rain-soaked and fresh, as if she had just stepped out of a cleansing downpour.

Jenna couldn't breathe. She had expected to see taunting, maybe invitation, in his eyes when she realized that he had been able to see her naked body as she'd changed. But what she saw was darker, harder. What she saw in those shimmering blue eyes was the same throb of desire she felt in her own chest. The struggle to keep distance, to prevent mistakes. The same kind of barriers, which were as formidable as hers.

Her hands moved up to his shoulders and into the silky hair on his collar, threading the strands through her fingers.

He cupped her cheek, his fingers sliding into her hair, holding her head steady while he explored the moistness of her mouth. "Sugar pie," he whispered gruffly, "you taste sweet, so sweet." In another devastating assault, he invaded her mouth. His touch had her tumbling into the sensation, plunging into the incredible pleasure.

She sucked in her breath when his hands traveled down her body and cupped her buttocks. Sliding his hand along one firm cheek, around to the back of her thigh, he leaned back, bringing her with him. His hand stopped at the underside of her knee as he cupped the delicate joint and lifted her leg.

"Yes..." Her voice caught as she felt the material of his pants against her inner thigh.

His breathing was ragged as he brought the softness of her mound against the hardness bulging in his trousers. She moaned softly against his mouth.

An abrupt knock on the door caused Jenna's eyes to fly open and her desire-drugged brain to realize where she was and what she was doing. She pushed on his chest, wondering how she could have lost her resolve like this.

Sam released her and backed up. "Just a moment," she called. "I'll be right there." She took a quick look in the mirror, hastily fixed her lipstick and tried to brush past him to open the door. Sam caught her around the waist and his hot, wet mouth slid across the back of her neck, the warmth of his kiss filling her with a heavy weakness.

She leaned back. "Sam, I have to open the door. Please."

"I know," he said in a whiskey-soft voice, and then he let her go.

As Jenna pulled open the door to greet the excited college students beyond, she realized that the fire her grandmother wrote about had never touched her.

Until now.

Now when she so desperately needed to focus on the task at hand.

She wasn't here for passion. Or was she? The fire beckoned with a sultry, dizzying dance full of promise. A promise that could draw her to that mesmerizing flame until she was engulfed.

What she wanted to know was, would she be able to escape once consumed?

4

THEY RODE IN SILENCE, but Jenna couldn't get that kiss out of her mind. She didn't dare look at him. Even in the darkness of his truck, she would be able to see his mouth. Unable to help herself, she turned, and the sight of his lips sent shivers of excitement over her skin.

His words drew her head around. "I was out of line. Way out of line."

He hadn't looked at her as he said it. Jenna knew it wasn't entirely his doing and in that knowledge she could be graceful. "It was spontaneous. Let's face it. When we get close to each other, there are some sparks."

He heaved a sigh. "And howdy."

"And if you greet every guest who visits Texas in that manner, I'm coming back."

He chuckled and turned to smile at her. Which, of course, didn't help one iota. It drew attention to his mouth, warm and soft, then hard and demanding. How would his mouth feel against her flesh, her breasts and between her legs? She squirmed in her seat, wishing they were already at the reception. He'd had to help her into the truck again. This time, she'd only shown a little leg when she'd placed her foot on the high running board, but Sam, ever the gentleman, had been there to boost her up and into the cab. She wished she'd worn a tight skirt so that he'd have to lift her up and hold her against him again.

When they reached the ritzy hotel where the reception was being held she quickly got out of the truck. Afraid if he put his hands on her she'd go up in flames.

He eyed her and held out his arm for her to link with his. But touching him would be a mistake, so she pretended she didn't see it and walked on ahead of him. When she entered the huge, bustling lobby, he was two steps behind her. Jenna didn't slow, not even to admire the elegance of the rich woodwork, or the mirrored columns and chandeliers. He'd offered his arm again.

There was a large easel in the lobby that held a poster of Jenna and, below it, the particulars of the location for the reception. She continued and had almost made it to the thick navy-blue carpet leading to the reception's ballroom, when she felt his warm hand on her arm.

"Whoa, darlin'. Where's the fire?"

Excitement exploded inside her as every nerve ending in her body screamed out in sensual agony. She gritted her teeth and took a quick breath and turned. "I didn't want to keep the guests waiting." She forced a smile, hoping that it didn't look forced.

He gestured to the painting in front of her. "I wanted to show you the portrait of my great-grandmother. As I mentioned, the town is named for her."

Jenna turned her attention to the portrait, glad to take her eyes off Sam. His great-grandmother, Savannah, was even more striking close up and Jenna could see some of the same facial characteristics in Sam. The same strong jawline, deep blue eyes and firm, sensuous lips. She almost groaned out loud.

His expression stilled and grew serious. "She was quite a lady. She helped my great-grandfather carve a life out of the wilderness, brought medicine to Savannah and founded the newspaper. She generally took care of the people in these parts up until she died."

He was proud of his heritage and he should be. His grandparents had built quite a nice little town. "And you're following along right in her footsteps by modernizing the hospital."

"Not a bad role model. I wished I'd gotten a chance to know her when she was young." He laughed. "Quite impossible, since I wasn't born yet."

Without warning, tears flooded her eyes and she turned away to hide them, but it was too late.

"I'm sorry. I reminded you of your grandmother."

"It's all right. It's still just so fresh. There are times when it hits me, when I remember she's really gone."

"I used to think of all these things, you know, in the course of the day, things I would normally save up to tell my dad. I'd think of something and go to pick up the phone to call him, and I couldn't because he was gone."

"Tell me it eases with time."

"It does."

She dabbed at her eyes with the handkerchief he handed her. "You're a good liar."

This was all she needed, this tender side of him, with his earnest face and the dark hair on his forehead, and those blue, blue eyes. Her eyes fell to his mouth—again.

"You keep doing that and we won't make it to the reception."

"Do what?"

"Stare at my mouth. It makes me crazy."

It makes me crazy. Her sentiments exactly. He made her crazy.

As they walked down the hall, music filtered out to them. They entered a large room filled with people, long tables draped with fine white cloths and piled high with sumptuous food. Three glittering chandeliers hung overhead. Numerous couples danced on the polished wooden floor to a soft tune.

Applause started somewhere and increased until everyone was clapping. Jenna was taken aback at the warmth in their eyes. Each person they passed offered their congratulations.

Jenna nodded after each person's words, flawlessly meeting and greeting people. Sam felt like a useless lump next to her, stung that she still wouldn't take his arm. The smile on his face began to hurt.

They moved farther into the room. A middle-aged woman with chin-length blond hair struck up a conversation. "You play beautifully. Where were you schooled?"

He eventually got pushed out of her circle and removed himself to get a drink. At the bar, he ordered whiskey straight up and threw the liquor back, emptying the shot glass. Ordering a glass of white wine and another whiskey, this time a double, he made his way back to her. Elbowing his way through, he handed Jenna the white wine. She smiled at him and brushed his hand with her fingers as she accepted it. For a split second, she hesitated, and then the heat in her eyes exposed her. He suddenly got it. She wouldn't touch him because she was attracted to him. That's why she wouldn't take his arm.

He caught snatches of the conversation.

"Do you travel to exotic places to play your music?" a woman in a shimmering black dress asked, sipping delicately from her champagne glass.

Jenna turned toward the woman, giving her a quick smile. Sam liked the way her face lit up as she answered the questions. "I'm on tour most of the year. I've been to Rome, Saint Petersburg and Budapest. I've done concerts at Christmas in London and New Year's Eve in Milan. They were all beautiful cities."

"How much do you have to practice every day?" asked a man dressed in a dark blue pinstripe suit, a new Stetson on his head.

Jenna shrugged. "It depends. If I'm learning a new piece, about four hours, otherwise, about two to three."

"What was it like to go to Julliard?" a dark-haired young woman asked, slipping her arm through her date's crooked one and leaning on his shoulder, dreams in her eyes. She smiled shyly. "I play the piano and hope to get into Julliard next year when I graduate."

"It was exciting and fun. I got to play my music every day, take dance and theater and even sing."

"You can sing? Let's hear a song." The girl's head lifted from the young guy's shoulder.

Jenna looked cornered and Sam muscled his way through again. "Look, she hasn't even eaten yet. Why don't you give her a chance to get a plate and jaw some more before you have her performing again?" He held out his hand and, like a lifeline, Jenna took it. A jolt of electricity shivered through him at her touch, but he held on.

He pulled her into his arms, thinking that dancing with her would give her time to catch her breath. He realized it only made him lose his.

"Do you always take charge?"

"When I see someone who I'm supposed to be hosting around town getting bombarded with questions and looking exhausted, I can't help but butt in."

She was staring at him and again her eyes were riveted to his mouth. "Is that true," he asked, "you travel most of the time?"

She drew her eyes away from his mouth and he felt a sense of relief. "Yes. I travel a good part of the year and practice the rest. It suits me."

"When do you have any fun?"

"Fun?"

"You know, things that make you relax and laugh. You do remember how to do that?"

She rewarded him with a smile. A very nice smile.

"I have vague memories of it."

"Well, while you're here, why don't we see if we can make some more memories?"

She blinked a couple of times and looked away as a faint rosiness deepened her skin. Well, he'd be damned. The city slicker blushed.

"You dance the waltz beautifully," she said, still not looking at him.

Immediately, memories of Tiffany badgering him into learning how to waltz stiffened his muscles. His walls came up and his barriers slammed into place. What the hell was he doing? Jenna's traveling reminded him too much of his own ex-wife's interest in getting away from the boredom of the ranch. He wasn't looking for another absentee woman. Their kiss was a lapse in judgment, a mistake that he could put down to libido and hormones. The woman was too fine for her own good, but that didn't mean he'd have to do anything about it. It would be better for everyone if he kept his distance.

"How about something to eat," he suggested as she let go of him, her face showing that she recognized the change in him. Hell, he couldn't help it. His ex-wife had shredded his heart, leaving him with an empty bed and an empty house.

He wanted to fill both with a woman who would stick around. It was the one thing that Jenna was not.

For hours she made her way through the room, deftly avoiding the spot where he was standing. She conversed with almost everyone. He watched her and still he wanted her. His own behavior unnerved him. His eyes followed her every move, and he felt this pull he couldn't identify, wasn't sure he wanted to identify. He wasn't accustomed to being irresistibly drawn to what he knew wasn't good for him and he didn't like it.

The orchestra was playing a heartrending tune that made him shift uncomfortably. The soft sounds seemed to intensify the foreboding that had been plaguing him all evening.

He'd screwed up royally by kissing her, he confessed. He was uncomfortable with the acknowledgment, and even more uncomfortable with the panic that welled up inside him at the thought. He'd never been this crazy about a woman before.

In the past twenty minutes of watching her, he was convinced she looked fatigued, something she was trying to hide. Maybe it was because he knew her a little bit better, albeit a couple days more, than these people. He wouldn't ever admit that he wanted to get to know her on a deeper level, a more intimate level. After she stumbled slightly, that was it. He moved from his spot and approached her. Taking her elbow, he said, "Say good-night."

She turned to look up at him. "I'm fine. It's still early."

"It's past midnight, Jenna."

"It is?"

"Yes, so say good-night. You're exhausted."

A group of students was moving in her direction. The same group that had managed to monopolize most of her time that night.

"Tell them you're leaving."

"I don't want to disappoint them. I can stay another half an hour."

He sighed, something stabbing at his heart. He

looked at the eager faces of the students and saw what she saw. Their awe, their hopes and dreams. It was all there on their faces. That she recognized it surprised him. That she cared shocked him for a moment. He hadn't expected that Jenna would care about anyone but herself, just as he'd expected her to sleep until noon and demand attendance by servants. How much else could he be wrong about?

He touched her arm. "You have that workshop and another concert. You'll have a chance to answer all their questions. Besides, I'm beat, too."

She stared at him. "You are? Of course, you are. What was I thinking? Just let me thank the Savannah College president and I'll be ready to leave."

Back in his truck the night streamed by as he drove them home. When he glanced over at Jenna, she had her eyes closed and her head lolled. She was tired, but it'd taken her another fifteen minutes to get out of the ballroom. Then she'd been stopped in the lobby by some of the townspeople to sign autographs, which took another fifteen minutes. Now it was past one and he was beginning to feel the fatigue across the back of his shoulders and deep in his muscles.

The problem was he'd have to be up at the crack of dawn to attend to the ranch chores. If he didn't clear some of the paperwork off his desk, he was going to be swimming in it up to his knees.

JENNA CAME TO with a start and realized it was because Sam had opened her door. She peered at him in the dim light.

"Come on, sleepyhead."

She rose and got as far as the running board before the blood rushing to her brain made her unsteady. With a soft cry, she wobbled forward only to be caught by two warm, strong hands at her waist. Still fighting for balance, she put out her hands and connected with his broad shoulders. She could feel the hard strength in him coiled and held in check in case she fell, but she didn't. He was a rock.

His hands tightened at her waist and the muscles bunched in his shoulders, making her stomach flutter at the power-packed flesh beneath her hands.

"One would think you weren't able to get into and out of a vehicle without help," he said with amusement.

"This truck is way too tall," she groused.

"Right, much taller than limos, I'm sure."

Her fuzzy brain couldn't get around that. Limos? She took taxis mostly to get where she wanted to go. Sure, sometimes she rode in a limo, but that wasn't the norm. She lost her train of thought as she looked down into his eyes, reflecting a thousand stars overhead. The inky, glittering beauty took her breath away.

Then she looked up into the heavens and gasped. The stars were so many and so bright. Living in the city, she hadn't realized how brilliant they shone. The movement of her head caused her to wobble again and he lifted her off the running board as gently and as easily as a dust mote.

"Let's get you down from there before you fall," he said with a flashing grin of white teeth.

"Right into your arms?" Her blood roaring in her

ears, she grinned back at him and felt a zing of danger. It settled into the pit of her stomach and tingled there. She liked the tingle.

Even though her feet hit the ground, his hands lingered at her waist. She liked that, too. He moved one big hand up and she thought that his hands looked too elegant for a rancher. He looked like he belonged in her world, playing the piano or holding the thin wood of a baton.

"I wouldn't mind," he said, his voice harsh and low, his thumb moving in a slow circle around her throat.

"Neither would I. I bet you're real good at catching people," she whispered. His light touch was magic, her nipples hardening beneath the flimsy material of her dress.

"Do you need catching?" Layers of meaning shaded his measured syllables. He cupped her neck.

"Maybe you should ask if I want to be caught."

The night wind lifted the leaves of the cedars, shades of gray off to her left. She could hear the whisper of wings on the air as night owls hunted for their prey. The shimmer of stars were gone from his eyes, but were replaced by a gleam that was so much more tantalizing the longer she plumbed the depths of his gaze.

She could imagine they were in some other place where he could lay her down and stroke her softly, endlessly until she whimpered and her eyes widened with need. Where she could see every nuance of his face, every pleasure-filled expression, see the light in those eyes burn brighter, hotter.

And then in that bright, clean place, he would burn inside her.

"Do you want to be caught?" he asked, tilting her face up to his.

"Maybe. Temporarily."

"Temporary suits me."

"It would have to, because my life is my music." She leaned into his touch. She knew what she *should* do, but his warmth was too enticing and she'd gone so long without that warmth.

He closed his eyes when her face moved insistently against his palm. "Music can't catch you."

"Sure it can, it always has. It always will."

He stilled, looking deeply into her eyes. "This is a warning?"

She realized it was. A warning that no matter what happened, music would have to come first. She knew when she was very young that she had to choose. Her gran had chosen love, but her mother had chosen music. Jenna would, too. It made her squirm inside to realize in that respect she was just like her mother. But the difference between them was that Jenna wouldn't use people. Her mother was a user. She manipulated and cajoled. Jenna preferred to take the straight tack. Even if it meant a head-on collision.

"When I have sex with a man, I like for him to know what I'm about."

"Are we going to have sex?"

"Every time you look at me, Sam, I feel ravished."

He groaned softly, leaning closer to her. He lowered his head. She lifted her chin. His mouth found hers, soft and willing.

She didn't mean for him to kiss her, not when she was strung-out with too little sleep and too much postconcert adrenaline jazzing up her insides, not when her guard was down and her hunger so powerful.

She kissed him back, tasting the answering hunger that had him driving her fast into passion, yet not fast enough for the hunger spiraling inside her.

Slanting his mouth across hers, he tugged at her lower lip, opening her mouth and deepening the kiss, tongue to tongue, stroking the innermost places.

She opened for him, his mouth warm and welcoming, inviting the sweep of his tongue.

She'd thought she'd only whimper with need.

Instead, his touch made her twist restlessly against him, one knee sliding up the side of his thigh, and he cupped her, pulling her into his rhythm, pulse to pulse in urgent, tearing need in the night.

And she found that this, after all, was what she wanted.

Him, against her, pushing her with each light touch of his hand. Her tucking her fingers into his waistband and dislodging his shirt as she brushed her knuckles against him, drowning in mindless dangerous sensation.

Jenna clung to him as if the world ended and began with Sam Winchester, exploded and recreated itself in his touch on her, hers on him.

She sighed in delight as Sam impatiently hooked his thumb into the silky material covering her breast and pulled the material away from her throbbing nipple.

Pushing her against the truck, he used his other

hand to shift the material up her legs until he could cradle himself in the vee of her legs, flush against her groin. He rocked his hips at the same time his hot, wet mouth engulfed her straining nipple. And he made her ache to have his touch on her, in her. Where he thrust, she yielded; where she retreated, he followed in a dance as old as time, as new as innocence.

Running her fingertips up the thick, well-defined muscles of his ribs, she flattened her hand against his skin. He buried his groan in the curve of her breast, his breath hot against her as he nipped the tip and held it between his teeth, the delicate pain trembling through her in an unending wave of shivers.

"Oh God, Jenna," he muttered against her breast, pulling her tight against him, taking her shivers and blending them with his shuddering response to the feel of her fingers. "I want you. God help me, but I want you so much it's killing me. Every time I touch you…"

And he took her mouth, gripping the sides of her head between his hands while the rough material of his jacket shot ripples of pleasure through her charged system. She lost all sense of anything except the drumming of her body against his, or his against hers—she no longer knew which. His flesh, hers, intertwined, humming with shared energy, both of them captive to that strumming beat.

She pulled her hand from his shirt and cupped him through the trousers he wore. He gasped against her, losing the measured rhythm of the kiss. She loved knowing his control was unraveling.

With his breath harsh and his lungs pumping, he

pushed against her hand in a mindless slide. Another low groan rumbled in his chest.

Somewhere in the deep recess of her mind where memories lived, she must have known this bliss of skin on skin and a man's dark, stubbled face against hers, this yielding to the mellifluous flow tingling through her.

But if her mind held such a memory, how could she have forgotten the experience? How would she have been able to separate herself from the thrilling buzz along her skin, the yearning to get beyond the silken barrier of skin to the core that beckoned?

Fear, like ice water, flooded her veins and she let go of him. Cupping his face, she brought it up to her. "You understand what this would be, right?"

He looked at her, confused, his eyes glazed. Her heart turned over. He looked so vulnerable she didn't want to say the words, but they had to be said. She couldn't have him believing there could be anything more. She couldn't bear to hurt him.

His eyes cleared and she smiled at the slash of wicked danger in the night.

"Sex, darlin'. Just sex. Is that what you want to hear?"

He drew away and tucked in his shirt and she wondered if he needed something to do with his hands so he wouldn't reach for her again.

"That's right. Not love, not friendship. Lust, sex, getting our groove on. Whatever you want to call it."

Jenna saw him retreat and part of her wanted to cry, but he had to be on the same page as she was. Her gran had wanted Jenna to read the diary to discover that this kind of passion was possible. Jenna realized now she'd found it, here in Sam's arms. She wanted it with him, but it had to be on her terms. He would have to agree.

"Damn, Jenna, you know how to kill the moment."

"Don't worry. I'll still respect you in the morning," she jeered, knowing that she would do more than that, but she couldn't let on.

His melting smile turned up the corners of his mouth. "That makes it easy on me. Temporary sex with a fancy city gal suits me just fine." His words were tough and struck hard, but she didn't buy them. The sound of his impassioned voice when he'd told her he wanted her made her heart tighten with an ache she'd never experienced before. He was using them as a defense mechanism. It was something she understood and accepted.

"That's all I can give."

"Tell you what, darlin', since you're trying so hard to convince me, why don't you decide when and where and let me know?"

She rearranged her dress just as she heard the scuff of boots on gravel.

"Sam. That you?"

Sam bent down, retrieved his Stetson and jammed it on his head. "Yeah, what is it, Tooter?"

She could hear the frustration in his voice.

"Just wanted to tell you it looks like the calving started, too. Black Beauty dropped a fine, strapping fella."

"Thanks, Tooter. Let's go have a look." He

grabbed Jenna's elbow and escorted her none too gently to the house. "I reckon you can make it from here."

She lifted her chin. "I reckon I can."

He was the kind of man who wasn't down for long. She could see it in the set of his broad shoulders. As easy and as lazy as a long, hot summer day, that smile had returned and, with it, a healthy dose of trouble.

"We're straight, city gal. But before you lay that pretty head down on your pillow tonight, why don't you think about the reason you're trying so hard not to like me?"

"I'm not trying that hard."

He laughed and she couldn't help herself, she was charmed down to her toes. Damn him, she wanted to kiss that laughing mouth.

So she did. Just grabbed the back of his neck, angled her head under the hat and kissed his startled mouth. Then she looked him in the eye. "Mmm, you are starting to grow on me," she said, before she licked her lips. She turned and sauntered into the house, smiling when she heard his very quiet, very fierce one-word epithet.

"Damn."

She made her way up the dim staircase to her designated room. Going over to the window, she watched him walk to the barn with Tooter. She was a fool. She had to relegate Sam as a distraction, a nuisance. The diary was her primary concern. Here she'd been in his home for two days and she still hadn't found even the desk, let alone the diary. Just when she thought she might have a chance to search the house, she saw Sam emerge from the barn. She stepped into the shadows, noticing how he glanced up at her window while he walked. Keep it light. Keep it shallow. She moved to the bed, weary and lonely. She'd just lie down for a moment and wait Sam out. He'd go to bed soon and when he did, she'd look for the diary. A sudden, desperate need to find her grandmother's legacy gripped her.

Her gran had talked about love and about time running out. For Jenna, her time ran out the moment she'd picked up the bow and dragged it across the strings of the violin.

A dedicated musician couldn't have both a loving family and a successful career. Her own family was proof enough.

Nope, she didn't want to get in over her head with Sam.

So why did it feel as if she were already drowning?

5

JENNA WOKE with a start, still in her dress and hose. She'd pulled the comforter over her in the night, so at least she hadn't been cold. She looked at the clock on the nightstand and saw that it was four o'clock. Her internal clock seemed to still be tuned to New York time.

She let herself drift and when she next opened her eyes, she saw that it was six o'clock. Pushing out from under the covers, she realized that she'd fallen asleep last night while waiting for Sam to do the same. She promised herself that today there'd be no more distractions. Jenna was no closer to discovering where Sam had placed her grandmother's rolltop desk than she was when she'd first arrived three days ago.

She stretched and reached back to unzip her dress, but the zipper caught and, no matter how she tugged, she couldn't get it free.

She slipped off the edge of the bed and walked to the door, hoping that Maria might be nearby. Jenna peered into the hallway and saw Sam come out of his bedroom. When he saw her, he froze.

She closed her eyes in mortification when he started forward. "Jenna?"

"Could you…" Her voice trailed off.

"Could I what?" he asked, walking over to her, an intrigued look on his face.

Jenna turned, closing her eyes. The heat of him permeated her clothing. She smelled the muskiness of his skin. She felt his desire like a tangible force. She felt the power of it, sensed his barely controlled passion. And she wanted, as she'd never wanted before. Just to lean into him to take the burden of her own desire off her shoulders. Just to let it go and see where it led her. But she couldn't, not now. She needed to have time alone to search his house. If she enticed him into her room, where would it lead? She could see herself spending the whole day in bed with this man.

She felt his hot breath against her ear. "What do you want, Jenna?" he whispered.

Her voice a hoarse rasp, she asked, "Could you please unzip my dress? I fell asleep with my clothes on last night. Now the zipper is caught."

"Sure. Is that all you need?"

His gentle fingers found the zipper and he fiddled with the tab, separating the fabric from the zipper's teeth. His fingers brushed her skin. She shivered and felt his body heat against her back like a lick of flame. He pulled the tab down her back. His fingers trailed along her spine in a tingling slide. They were strong, masculine hands that were very good at holding a woman, stroking, caressing. Every touch seemed intimate beyond her belief.

"That's all I need for now," she replied.

The need flared in her, hot and urgent. His lower body pressed up against her softly rounded buttocks.

His heat scorched her. She could feel the hardness of his arousal press into her. An ache tied her stomach in knots, sent a rush of heat over her exposed skin and sparked a fire that began to burn.

He lifted her heavy hair off her left shoulder, pushing the mass aside. Then she felt his lips on the curve of her neck and heat burst through her. Right now everything seemed as it should be. God help her, but she desired him, his touch, his body. His mouth moved to the top of her shoulder and he very softly kissed her exposed skin.

His hand settled at her waist and she reached down and covered his hand.

"I never did tell you last night how beautifully you play." He whispered against her ear, sending prickles of heat stabbing into the tips of her breasts.

Gently she squeezed his hand. "Thanks." His breath gusted out. She released his fingers, and he removed his hand.

His fingertips brushed along her scalp, sending little prickles of heat into her neck as he gathered her hair in his hands and smoothed it down her back.

"Are you on your way out to do chores?"

"I have to get into the hayloft today and tidy up. I have meetings this afternoon with the Savannah Hospital fund-raising group." He was silent for a moment as if weighing his next words. "Would you like to come?"

The seductive cadence to his voice made her almost want to agree with everything he said. She took a deep, shuddering breath. Joy leaped inside her. It would give her ample time to search. "Sounds like you'll be busy all day. I'm sorry, so will I. I have a reception with the faculty and chair of the music department at one o'clock at Savannah College along with a rehearsal at three. I have to get in some practice time today, as well.''

She clasped her hands together, desperately needing something to do with them or she'd soon have them all over his enticing, hard-muscled body.

Unabashed and unapologetic, she escaped. There was no other word for the way she scampered away from him, gave him a quick smile and shut the door.

Was it because she wanted the morning to find the desk or was it because he unnerved her like no other man ever had? Made her insides curl into knots and her heart beat hard and uneven. Or was she just being...well, practical?

Maybe not. Practical women knew how to retreat gracefully.

Cowards knew when to run and Jenna had been running as she backed away from the door. She shucked her dress, her hose, and hotfooted it for the safety of the bathroom before she did something really foolish like throw the door open, grab Sam and slake her desire with the hardness of his body.

The water was steaming hot and relaxing as she sighed beneath its spray. She was determined to get to that desk this morning and remove the diary. Then she could go to her events this afternoon secure in the knowledge that she'd fulfilled her gran's dying wish.

Guilt stabbed at her when she realized she'd barely thought of Gran in the past twenty-four hours. Gran had been a staunch supporter for as long as Jenna could remember. It used to pain her that her mother only breezed through her life. Her disappointment and dislike of her mother had never left her. It'd been hard for a five-year-old to take, but now she had learned to live with her mother's behavior, and realized that love and music couldn't mix. One had to lose. It was the same with her gran. Susanna had left the opera for her husband and tiny granddaughter. Jenna thanked God every day for her gran's sacrifice.

Jenna had no intention of letting her feelings get in the way of her music career. She was at the height of her fame and she intended to stay there as long as she could. Music was a safe pursuit. She understood it, unlike the emotions of desire and need, which were confusing and always led to a loss of control.

The second time she opened her door that morning it was quiet in the house. Sam was at the barn and it was still very early. She glanced at Sam's bedroom door, wondering if the desk could be inside. Taking a deep breath, she crossed the hall and turned the knob. The door swung open on silent hinges.

She stepped inside the sunny room. Her eyes roamed over the simple cedar furniture, the big double bed with a colorful Native American comforter, a dresser and a nightstand. Near a window, a big overstuffed chair sat, and beyond were the pastures where longhorn cattle grazed.

No rolltop desk, and that should have been the end of it. Yet she couldn't bring herself to leave.

She went to the dresser and scanned the contents: a man's very old pocket watch, a simple star with a circle and some loose change. Jenna picked up the watch and examined the silver timepiece. It was a priceless antique. Jenna had been around them enough in her life to know one when she saw it. She pushed on the winder. The faceplate snapped up, revealing the clock beneath. Inside, the inscription read, To My Beloved Husband, Silas, with All My Heart. Love, Savannah.

The personal words made her realize that she was snooping through Sam's private belongings. Appalled at herself but unable to stop, she gently closed the timepiece.

Next, she picked up the star and easily identified it as a Texas Ranger badge. Bringing it close to her eyes, she could see that around the circle it read, Department of Public Safety, Texas Rangers, Company A. Sam was a man with a rich past, just like Jenna, who had the burden of her gran's scandalous diaries.

Perhaps a man like Sam would understand if Jenna just explained to him how important her gran's mementos were to her. Except she remembered her expectation that a judge would understand the legalities of an illegally auctioned desk and return all items found in that desk. She couldn't take the chance.

She approached the bed and imagined his big body sprawled there among the blankets and pillows and her stomach jumped. She ran her hand over the footboard, carved with the skull of a longhorn, the long, thin horns reaching from one end to the other. Belts and chaps were draped over one corner, along with the white shirt he'd worn to the concert. Stepping around the numerous boots in jumbled disarray at the foot of the bed, she reached out and snagged the shirt, bringing it to her nose. She was used to sweet-smelling men, but Sam didn't wear cologne. He didn't need the artificial scent. Breathing deep, she took in the wonderful, enticing fragrance of Sam.

She closed her eyes and savored the aroma. It was like no other: leather, wind, soap, raw and all-consuming.

The front door slammed and Jenna heard quick footsteps cross the foyer and start up the stairs. She hooked the shirt back on the post and headed for the door. She made the threshold just as Maria came to the foot of the stairs.

Jenna stepped through the open door. She could hardly believe she'd been going so thoroughly through his things. A blush rushed into her cheeks.

"If you're looking for Sam, he's in the barn. I saw him when I dropped Cal off twenty minutes ago. I'm way behind schedule because of that talkative Tooter. Would you mind telling Sam breakfast will be served in a jiffy?"

Jenna smiled and tried to ease her fast-beating heart. "I'd be happy to. Thanks."

She headed for the stairs as Maria went into his bedroom. Jenna could see her gathering up his dirty clothes. She sighed, her only thought was that Sam's shirt would get washed.

Halfway to the barn, Jenna started to get nervous, feel as if she'd gotten a glimpse into Sam's soul. The star and the pocket watch said so much about him and she hungered for more.

"Sam, are you in here?" The floor of the loft above squeaked, and hay and dirt rained down.

When he came into view, he was naked from the waist up, except for a blue bandanna tied around his strong throat. His dark hair lay thick and wet against the back of his neck.

The black Stetson sat on his head, she presumed to keep the hair off his face, the brim pulled down so that his intense eyes were in shadow. Shadow that kissed the sleek line of his bare arms and pooled in the hollow of his throat.

All that was visible was the stubble on his cheeks and chin, which only accentuated his chiseled lips and strong cheekbones. Well-used brown leather gloves covered his hands for protection.

Her words dried up. She was struck dumb and all she could do was stare. She watched as a trickle of perspiration slid down his chest, over the taut muscles of his stomach to soak into the already wet waistband of his jeans. Jenna licked her lips, almost able to taste the sleek saltiness of his skin.

He crouched and lowered his voice. "What's the matter, darlin'? Cat got your tongue?"

She watched the soft beaten denim stretch and remembered the heavy muscles of Sam's thighs as he had straddled her the night before. Her voice came out hoarse. "No. Just got a little bit of dust in my eyes."

She couldn't help watching him, her eyes roaming over the sleekness of his chest.

He hesitated, his blue eyes flashing in the semi-darkness of the barn.

Sam put his hands on the edge of the loft's floor. With a deft turn, he swung his body off the lip and let himself drop down to the hay below, landing securely on his black-booted feet.

Sam strode, then stopped just inches from her. Heat radiated off him. The musky smell of him made for a heady combination.

His eyes caressed her face and she knew that her desire for him was written there. So easy for him to read.

He stripped off the gloves and moved close to her. "Let me see that dust."

He stuck the gloves in his back pocket and leaned even closer. Instinctively she reached out to steady herself and her hand came into contact with his wide chest. His breathing quickened as he peered into her eyes. His hands came up to her face and she flinched suddenly.

"Steady," he murmured in a coaxing voice he probably used on his horses and longhorns. His hands were rough and callused from hard work. How could they be so gentle? Jenna ached with the comfort of his hand on her face, with the warmth of his breath on her forehead, stirring the fine strands at her hairline. She could feel the steady strength of his heartbeat beneath her hand where it lay against moist, hard flesh.

He frowned slightly and said, "They look fine to me. You telling me stories?"

She gulped, desperate for composure, knowing she wasn't going to find it with him standing so close. "Okay, I lied. I was a little taken aback by your lack of attire. You don't see many males running around like that in New York.''

''My lack of…well, shoot. Does it bother your delicate sensibilities?''

''No.''

''No? So it doesn't bother you?''

''Yes.''

''It does.''

''Not really…Sam, you're confusing me.'' She closed her eyes, hoping, praying for composure.

He smiled and stepped closer. ''Want me to put on a shirt?''

''No…I mean, yes.''

He crowded against her. ''What is it? Yes or no?''

''You are exasperating. Your body doesn't offend me.'' She took a deep breath. ''I came down here because I thought you might be hungry and Maria's about to serve.''

''I know all about hunger, Jenna. The kind that burns in my gut every time you look at me like you're doing right now.''

Jenna, feeling trapped, tried to take the upper hand. ''Sam, are you going soft on me?''

Her words died as he slipped his arm around her waist, his forearm tightening against her lower back. Dragging in a ragged breath, he pulled her against him. ''Darlin', there isn't anything *soft* about me right now.''

His hot mouth came down on hers. He was right. Everything about him was hard—his muscles, his demanding mouth, his grim determination, and the part of him that was pressed tightly to her.

His lips were like warm, moist velvet. She shivered and groaned as his hot mouth closed over hers, so seductively gentle that she leaned into him, heedless of involving her heart, heedless of the consequences. Heedless of her own doubts, her arms went around his neck, knocking the Stetson to the barn floor. Her hands cupped the back of his head, delving into the damp raw silk of his hair. With a soft growl in his throat, he deepened the kiss, his tongue darting into her mouth like a hungry flame that burned hotly yet so sweetly.

Sam pulled away. He closed his eyes, his face belying the struggle waging within himself. His body shook beneath her hands, evidence of the powerful emotions that were locked inside him.

She touched his face. His eyes opened, and the vulnerability she saw there once again made her heart ache. This Sam scared her. She liked it better when he used that slow-simmering cowboy charm on her. This open, yearning Sam was alarming and, she had to admit, thrilling.

For a full minute, he looked down into her face. His free hand came up and he pressed his thumb along her bottom lip. Jenna groaned, her head falling back. She let out a long sigh when he traced her upper lip.

"Ever done it in the hay?" he whispered. Cupping her face in his hands, he lowered his lips, barely touching her mouth, teasing and tempting her with wispy, nipping bites and a soft brushing. Her breathing quickened when his tongue snaked out and touched her mouth. He tasted rich, dark and forbidden. Without any further urging from her, he once again closed his hungry mouth over hers.

Her knees buckled and he caught her around the waist, dragging her against his hard body. "Now, darlin'?" he murmured. "How about now?"

She didn't have time to respond as his mouth closed over hers again. It was a shock to her that hunger could be so luscious, that domination could taste so sweet. He brushed her lips lightly, a slow slide, his mouth as gentle as the kiss of morning dew. His hand twined into her hair, lifted a strand and let it cascade through his fingers. His eyes were lit from within by an intense, tangible fire. And then he stopped playing games and plundered her mouth, bruised with a fervor that astounded Jenna to the depths of her soul, that ignited a hot flood of desire Jenna never recognized she possessed. She met him, succumbed to him, danced with him in a honeyed waltz of desire and need.

Jenna dissolved into his sizzling touch, into his heady scent and harsh moans. His mouth moved over her as if he couldn't get enough and she offered her own sigh of surprise. Heat scorched from his fingertips and crackled from his mouth. Fascination coalesced to craving, sweeping away resistance. Jenna arched against him, her breasts aching for the brush of him. She tortured her own fingers with the silky mantle of his hair and partnered her tongue with his. And when she felt his hand drop to cup her breast, she knew that this was what her grandmother had been talking about.

Passion.

She burned with it like an incandescent flame. She knew that if she didn't grab this time with Sam, she might not find this perfect harmony, this intense meshing ever again.

He cradled her against the sleek, tough contours of his chest.

He pulled his mouth away from hers, his breathing ragged, his eyes dilated. She was struck by how thick and long his eyelashes were. His dark, hungry gaze bored into her.

"Sam?" Tooter's voice filled the entrance to the barn.

"Damn," he muttered, and let her go. "I guess we'll have to make hay some other time. Damn," he said again, his voice harsh. He stepped away from her, pulled the gloves out of his back pocket and slid them on, using the simple task to compose himself. Jenna tried, but all she wanted to do was get her hands on Sam. "Go on up to the house and I'll be up shortly. Tell Maria she can serve in thirty minutes. Can you wait that long?"

"I don't think I can wait much longer," she said quietly, but didn't give Sam time to say anything as she walked past him. When she saw Tooter, she started to give him an easy smile, but the old man only glared at her as he passed. She stopped and turned to look at his retreating back. Oh, so that was the way it was going to be. The old man kept inter--rupting them on purpose. She wondered what he had against her personally. When she got a moment, she'd ask Sam. She was accustomed to people liking her and it bothered her that such a nice old man didn't.

"SAM?"

"Back here, Tooter."

When the old man came into view, Sam had completely composed himself. Although his blood still pumped heavily through his system, outwardly he was calm. "What is it?"

"The fella with the feed is here."

"Tooter, why are you bothering me with this?"

"Thought you'd want to know."

Sam faced off with the foreman, irritated, frustrated, furious. "That's interesting, because ever since you were hired on this ranch which was, what, *more than twenty years ago,* you've been handling the *feed fella* without letting me know a damn thing about it."

Tooter shuffled his feet and glared right back at him, just as frustrated. He definitely looked like a man who had something powerful on his chest.

"Does this have to do with keeping me and Miss Sinclair apart?"

Tooter scowled mightily. "She's no good for you, Sam. You can't see beyond your hormones. She's just like the ol' missus."

Heat suffused Sam's chest, mostly because he knew Tooter was right. She was too much like his ex-wife, but at this moment, he just didn't care. He wanted her. "What I do or don't do with Miss Sinclair is my business. I don't need you handling me, Tooter. Just do the job I pay you for."

The sudden anger deflated the moment Sam saw the hurt on the old man's face. Sam bent down and picked up his fallen hat, slicked his hand impatiently through his hair and jammed the hat back on his head.

"Look, I'm sorry. That was uncalled-for, but what I'm trying to say is that I'm a grown man and I know what I'm doing."

"Do you? I saw the way you were looking at her yesterday when I came to tell you about Black Beauty. I might not be as young as I once was, but I'm not blind."

"Don't try to tell me how to run my life. I value your opinion, Tooter, but not in this instance."

Tooter shot him a sardonic look. "You're hot for that little filly and she'll break your heart."

"It's temporary and it'll wear off after she's gone."

"Can't be soon enough for me. The moment I saw her I knew dust was gonna kick up."

Tooter whirled and marched off, grumbling about stupidity and hormones. Sam wasn't sure he didn't agree with him.

He clenched his gloved hands and turned and quickly made his way back up to the loft. He could still feel the imprint of her hand on his face, the way she'd looked up at him, all soft and melting. Her fingers were long and graceful, fingers made to hold and coax such beautiful music out of a wooden stringed instrument. But Sam wanted to taste those fingers. He wanted to feel them on his skin. He wanted to find himself so immersed in her that he could forget everything, everyone. Who he was and who she was.

But he knew better. He'd known better all along.

Tooter was right. She didn't belong here. She belonged in New York City, where men kept their clothes on in public. She belonged in a place where sleek skyscrapers hugged a magnificent skyline, traffic honked and moved at a snail's pace. A place where sophistication was an everyday occurrence. Not a place where there was dust, mud, hay and sweat.

He was raw, rough and tough, but the moment she looked at him with her soft brown eyes, he was lost.

Later, Tooter could say he'd told Sam so. Much later.

6

UNSETTLED BY HIS FIGHT with Tooter, Sam stopped in the closest bathroom to wash his hands.

He had nothing but the deepest respect for his foreman. Tooter was the only other person on the face of the earth that knew how far Sam's father had sunk into alcoholism. Tooter had covered for Sam's father whenever he would binge. He would run the ranch until Sam's father sobered up, until the next time.

Sam couldn't blame his father for his addiction. He had suffered terrible losses with his first son stillborn and his wife dying while birthing his second son.

That knowledge didn't make Sam any less lonely, though. But Tooter had gone a long way in alleviating a lot of the feelings of resentment and isolation. He'd taken Sam under his wing and taught him everything there was to learn about running a place like the Wildcatter.

It made him unhappy that Tooter didn't like Sam having a personal relationship with Jenna. But he wasn't going to stop pursuing her. Quite frankly, he wanted to have sex with her and was determined to get the woman in his bed.

When he was finished, he headed for the dining

room, but just as he passed the door to the game room, he saw Jenna.

He stopped and came into the room. Jenna was looking around as if she was searching for something. Something important by the expression on her face. She had her back to him and was dressed in a pair of black leggings and a short lime-green T-shirt that ended at her waist. When she moved, the smooth skin of her midriff peeked out. The tight black pants cupped her bottom, making him want to slide his hands along the sultry curve. The thick braid down her back brought him the memory of how the strands had felt against his fingers. How she had shivered against his touch.

"What are you doing in here? Don't tell me you like to play pool?" He meant it in a teasing way, but she started and turned to face him. Her expression blanched and she looked at him with such a guilty expression that his Ranger instincts snapped on.

"I got lost," she blurted out, then she laughed nervously. "Went to the bathroom and must have taken the wrong way back to the dining room."

Sam studied her face and frowned. Jeez, he was getting paranoid. From the obvious blush on her cheeks, she was embarrassed about getting lost. Of course, he had a big house. It was understandable that she wouldn't be familiar with the ins and outs of the place.

He took her arm. "The dining room is this way." She followed him back down the hall and into the dining room. He pulled a chair out for her and she sat.

Sam took his seat and Maria came into the room with two plates. She placed one plate in front of Jenna and another in front of him. "I've got to do the shopping, Sam. I'll be gone for about an hour."

"I have meetings in town, so I won't be here. Would you mind driving Miss Sinclair to the college for me? I'll have one of the hands pick her up when she's finished."

"Sure, my pleasure."

"Thanks, Maria," Sam said as she left the dining room.

Orange juice in a glass pitcher and a coffee carafe sat on the table. Sam reached for the coffeepot. "Coffee?"

Jenna nodded. "Thanks," she said when he'd filled her cup.

Sam's cell phone rang and he answered. "Winchester. Yes, Tooter, I am. How much are we over? Sure, I'll stop by the feed store on the way back home and let them know." He ended the call and proceeded to pour the coffee.

She wondered if Tooter was looking for reasons to interrupt Sam while he was with her. She couldn't forget the look Tooter had given her in the barn. "Why is Tooter mad at me?"

Sam bobbled the coffee carafe and sloshed steaming liquid on the table. He wiped at it with his napkin.

"He's temperamental."

He watched as she brushed her braid back over her shoulder. "He wasn't temperamental until he saw us together last night."

"He thinks you're a lot like my ex-wife and that

getting involved with you is a bad idea.'' Tooter was dead right. It was a bad idea, but it'd be a few days of hot sex, then she'd be gone.

"Am I?'' She forked up eggs and chewed.

"Are you what?''

She selected strawberry jam, picked up a spoon and put a dollop of jam on her toast. "Like your ex-wife. Tiffany, isn't it?''

"Yes, her name is Tiffany.'' He speared some chucks of scrambled eggs with his fork and took a bite.

"So, am I?'' She slathered the jam on the toast and took a delicate bite.

"In some ways.''

Her eyebrows arched and her voice rose in mild surprise. "What ways?''

"Tiffany liked to travel. She used it as an excuse to get off the ranch and get away from me.'' He was suddenly distracted when she used her tongue to retrieve some jam at the corner of her mouth. Pink and darting, the sight of it tantalized him. He realized that she was waiting for him to finish. "She was very interested in the ranch when I met her at a honky-tonk after a stock show in Dallas. She's from Boston originally and I think she thought the cowboy life was glamorous.''

She finished up the eggs on her plate but left the steak and potatoes. "Until she had to live on the ranch?'' She reached over and picked up her coffee and took a sip.

"Right. She hated it and found many excuses to leave until one time she didn't come back.'' He took a mouthful of eggs, realizing that time was getting short and he had to get into the shower. He cut the steak and followed the eggs with a bite.

"I'm sorry, Sam."

He shrugged. "It's in the past." And it was. He no longer wondered or worried about Tiffany. She'd never really loved him and he sometimes wondered if it was what she represented more than who she was that had enticed him into marriage.

"At least you had a marriage. I've never even seriously dated. How can you tell a guy that, sure, I'd love to go out with you right after I get back from this six-month tour?" He was sure she didn't mean to let the loneliness show, but it did. It was etched in her face, mirrored in her eyes and his heart stumbled.

"Yeah. I guess that puts a damper on getting close to someone."

"Gives him plenty of time to make reservations, though." She gave him a teasing smile and Sam laughed, but it was muted because this time his heart tightened.

Her eyes softened and she gave him an intimate look full of warmth and amusement. Her gentle look made him realize he'd never experienced this kind of moment with his ex-wife. He wanted to touch Jenna in ways that would make her gasp and cry out. There wasn't just loneliness there, but steel and a toughness that surprised him. He wanted to make the loneliness go away and make the toughness unnecessary.

"So now I understand why you were a little put off when we first met. You thought I'd come to the ranch and be unhappy when I found out it wasn't *glamorous.* You didn't want me in your way. That's what happened with the crack-of-dawn-drag-me-out-in-the-rain tour of the barn. To give me a taste, so I'd get out of your hair?''

"Guilty."

"You didn't expect me to enjoy it."

"You did?"

"Yes. The rain made everything fresh and I found I liked the smell of hay and warm horses."

"It was an underhanded thing to do, but..."

"You enjoyed every minute."

He laughed. "I did until you burst my bubble and told me you always get up early." How could she turn him inside out like this? All that sweet fragrance and her delicate curves. More than that, though. Her essence—that was what pulled him. Something in her nature that sang to him like a siren song, pulling him off his horse, and right into knife-sharp thorns.

They sat there for a moment in silence, then Jenna picked up her plate.

"You don't have to do that. Maria will take care of this when she gets back."

"Don't be silly. It's only a few dishes. It'll take a second to bring them into the kitchen."

She grabbed the orange juice pitcher in the other hand and left the room. Sam took a few more quick bites and picked up his plate, the jam and the carafe.

He was just in time to see Jenna's tight backside sidle over to the fridge to deposit the pitcher on a shelf. When the door opened, the plastic mustard container slipped off the inner door shelf and hit the floor with a soft plop. As she bent over, he lost his train of thought. It went out of his head like mist.

Her short T-shirt exposed a large expanse of skin. The heavy braid swung down, hanging in the air. He remembered how each silky strand had felt, how her hot mouth had consumed him. Sam grew hard, hot.

He was pretty sure she wanted him. The signals she sent him couldn't be misconstrued. But she had doubts and he wanted her to understand that she could have everything on her own terms. Somehow he sensed that was important to her.

It was important to him to taste her, hold her, take her, as he wanted. He'd agree to anything.

She straightened, replaced the mustard container and shut the door. Picking up her plate, she scraped the remainder of breakfast into the sink and turned to grab his plate right out of his hands. He wanted her. The thought became an overpowering urge, but not now. Not here in the kitchen when he had things to do and she did, too.

She ran water, added soap and quickly washed the plates. Sam set down the carafe and placed the jam in the fridge. He went back for the cups and saucers and the silverware. When he got back, he placed all the dirty dishes in the water and picked up a dishtowel to start drying. He had other things he should be doing, but he couldn't bear to leave her. Her musician's hands knew how to do more than hold an instrument.

"You don't have a housekeeper?"

"No. I don't need one. I live in an apartment in the city. I have someone come in to clean, but that's it."

"So I guess I'm a bit more pampered than you are."

He set each piece of crockery on the counter as she drained the water.

He draped the damp towel along the sink.

"Sam, you can't compare what I do and what you do. I don't do physical labor from morning to dusk and have a ton of paperwork waiting for me in the evening. I practice, rehearse and, in the evenings, I play."

"It's ironic that I thought you had someone to wait on you hand and foot and here it is me who has that."

"When would you find time to cook, clean and do your wash?"

"That's a good point, but doesn't let me off the hook now, does it?"

"Okay, so you were ignorant of my lifestyle and made assumptions about me. You're forgiven." She opened cupboards until she found the right one for the plates. She reached up to place the plates with the other clean ones.

He couldn't take the time to make love to her, but it didn't mean he couldn't touch her. He slid the back of his knuckles along her rib cage. Her quick intake of breath gave him intense pleasure as the plates came down a little too hard.

She turned to him. "Sam." His name came out a strangled plea.

Sam wrapped her braid around his hand and drew her closer. "I know. We have things to do today and I did say that I'd wait until you were ready, but I can't help myself.'' Her hair was so soft against his palm. He drew her closer.

"How can I argue with you, when I feel the same,'' she said, resting her hand against his chest. She slipped her arms around his neck and for a moment they held on to each other.

With Sam against her like this, her body trembled. She had to keep her wits about her. It would be much faster if she got him to show her where the desk was, so she could search it later. "How about a tour of the house before you go, so that I don't get lost again.''

"Sure.'' He let her go and led her out of the kitchen. He took her back through the dining room and into the hall that led to the game room, pointing out closets and bathrooms, gesturing toward the pool area, which Jenna could see as they passed the game room.

He took her to the back of the house and, at a set of double doors, stopped. "This is my office. I'm in the process of having it remodeled, so, sorry about the mess.''

Jenna walked in and immediately noticed the disarray, but the roaring in her ears drowned out Sam's words. For against the far wall and partially draped with a white sheet was her gran's shining mahogany rolltop desk. And the sight made her pulse jump and her heart begin to pound.

"I should mention that the contractor will be in and out of the house. They're waiting for the crown molding and as soon as that comes in, he'll be able to finish up.''

Jenna barely heard what he had to say. Every nerve

ending in her body was quivering. She wanted to get to the desk.

"Jenna? Are you okay?"

She jerked her head around and looked at him. "Yes. I was just admiring your beautiful desk—what I can see of it."

Sam walked over to the desk and pulled off the drape. "Isn't she a beauty? I've been searching for one just like it for years."

"It looks like an antique. Where did you get it?"

"I got this at an auction when I was in New York a few weeks back. It was made in the 1880s. Belonged to a deceased opera singer. I wonder where she found it?"

Jenna knew exactly where her gran had gotten the desk. They had been in Houston on an antique buying trip when gran had seen an estate sale in the paper. That was where they had found this desk.

It looked ten times better than when she'd seen it last. Sam had restored the wood surface and had the rolltop repaired. It was quite a beautiful piece of furniture. And a treacherous one, for inside lurked possible scandal for men she didn't know, along with her gran and anyone else associated with the diary and the jewelry.

Maybe she could tell him, right now. Ask him if she could look through the desk and remove what was hers. But what if he refused? What if he said no and then became angry at her deception? Could she take that chance?

The clock in the office chimed the hour and Sam threw the drape back on the desk. "Damn, look at the time. I've really got to go.'' He waited until Jenna was out of the double doors before he closed them. She was relieved to see he didn't lock them. She didn't need that impediment. She followed him through the house and up the stairs.

"I hope we can have dinner together tonight," he said as he took her hand, then looked at it in surprise. "Jenna, your hand's like ice."

She was chilled. Chilled that she had to lie to Sam, who really seemed like a decent man, but again she couldn't risk it. She felt the heat from his big hands engulf hers and she smiled up into his concerned face. "It'll be fine. I'm going to practice and my hands always warm to the strings. Go take your shower before you're late. You've already spent enough time entertaining me."

"Not nearly enough," he said, letting her go. "I enjoy your company."

She felt guilt surface inside her. It was an emotion she hadn't expected. She could at least tell this much of the truth. "I enjoy yours, too."

He turned and disappeared into his room and Jenna moved to her door. Entering, she left the door ajar so she could see when Sam passed. She pulled a chair next to the window, picked up her violin case and set it on the bed. The gleaming Stradivarius caught the sunlight from the window, blinding her for a moment. She took out the bow and examined the bow hairs, picked up the rosin and applied it generously to the bow until she was satisfied.

She heard the water go on in Sam's bathroom and glanced up, momentarily distracted by the thought of him naked and under the spray as she'd been only hours before.

Hard, thick muscle and warm, wet skin and the exciting smell of him. She wasn't going to leave this house until she'd had her full taste of that passion Gran had described in her diary. She wanted to wrap herself around Sam until she blended with him, pulled from him the music of ecstasy with the strength of her hands. She looked down at her fingers wrapped around the bow. It would only be a taste of passion, though, because her music eclipsed everything.

Jenna lamented that she didn't have more friends outside the music business, felt regret that she wouldn't marry or mother children. The fire inside her to perform burned with a fervor that she couldn't overcome. She closed her eyes and admitted to herself that, in that realization, she was her mother's daughter. Selfish and unwilling to let anything intrude. Oh, there were subtle differences. Where her mother embraced fame, sought it out and nurtured it, Jenna accepted it for what it was, and understood that it was necessary for her to be allowed to continue to play. To express herself in the lilting chords of music, the flow of the bow, the vibration of the instrument, the feel of the wood against her skin.

Where her mother wanted worship, Jenna wanted only to perform. Where her mother took from people and hurt them beyond repair, Jenna shunned intimacy, unwilling to subject another living soul to her obsession with her music.

It was true she'd found herself alone most of her life. She'd filled those hours with a companion that couldn't leave her or hurt her, because it was an inanimate object. Her true talent lay, not in the instrument, but in herself. And, in that self-containment, she felt secure.

She walked to the door with the bow in her hand and looked at Sam's room. It wasn't that she couldn't care about him—she could, deeply. It was that she wouldn't let herself, wouldn't let him into her life because hers was given over to the music.

And she would not see him a burned-out, twisted, empty hulk of a man, as her father had been before he'd disappeared from her life. Love was a powerful and intense enemy, but Jenna would fight against it with all she had. Sam needed a woman who wanted to stay put and give him children. To embrace the ranching life and everything he was. Jenna couldn't. Her life was her concerts and one city after another.

Her life *was* the music.

The water turned off and she heard his bathroom door open. Earlier, he'd shut the door to his bedroom, but it hadn't latched. In the gap between the jamb and the edge of the bedroom door, she could see him toweling himself off, oblivious to her eyes.

Her mouth went dry at the rousing sight of him. Sleek muscles delineated from tough physical work, ripples of steel through his thighs from hours in the saddle, a flat washboard stomach, thick, wide chest, broad shoulders and arms that really knew how to hold a woman.

Unprepared for the sudden desire that stabbed through her, Jenna leaned into the doorjamb for support. She'd never been so aroused by simply looking at a man.

But Sam was so much more than a body. He had quick intelligence and a wry sense of humor, responsibility to a town that was his own special, cherished legacy, courage and strength and a gentleness that brought tears to her eyes.

He used the towel on his hair and rubbed it with vigor, just as he did all things, with an intense, contained energy that must vibrate through him.

He disappeared from her sight, but then was back, his hair neatly combed off his face. His upper body disappeared and then reappeared as he stepped into a pair of black briefs, then black socks. Then the black dress pants, the silky electric-blue T-shirt that hugged the contours of his chest. Efficient and confident, he slipped a black belt through the loops in the pants, twisting his upper torso until he buckled it over his groin. He pulled on a pair of shiny black boots. With a quick shrug, he slipped into the Western-cut coat and grabbed the black Stetson.

She retreated away from the door as he disappeared from sight again. She could only imagine he was grabbing his wallet, putting on his watch and slipping that loose change into his pocket with those maddening, graceful hands.

She heard his footsteps as he left the room. He glanced in just as she put the bow to the violin. Waving casually, he smiled. ''Have a good day.''

When she acknowledged him with a little smile, he angled his head and held her hostage for a few extra seconds. The bright shirt intensified the color of his eyes. Eyes she could get lost in, she thought, as he broke eye contact. In two strides he was across the room, cupping her face, leaning down and kissing her. His scent filled her as she closed her eyes and absorbed every sensation. He broke the kiss and then he was gone.

She waited until she heard the front door slam. Placing the violin and bow back in the case, she walked to the window and saw him get into his truck after a quick wave to Cal, who was bringing a magnificent black stallion out of the barn.

His truck disappeared over the rise. She walked silently back to the office. But at the sound of a vehicle, Jenna froze. Had Sam forgotten something? She rushed back to the front of the house and had her foot on the first step of the stair when there was a loud knock on the door.

Jenna hesitated, turned and walked into the foyer. Through the glass, she could see three men waiting outside. She opened the door and the tallest one smiled at her. "Sam or Maria?"

"Both of them are gone."

"No problem. I'm Jake Stanton and these are my two sons. The crown molding came in finally and we're here to finish Sam's office. We'll try to keep the noise down to a minimum."

Frustration and disappointment filled her chest. Damn, when was she going to get a break? She tried to appear unruffled and graciously opened the door the rest of the way. "I'll be leaving soon myself, so your noise won't bother me."

Just then, Maria's car appeared in the distance and Jenna knew that there was no use trying to search the desk during the day. She'd have to give it a shot tonight.

7

October 10, 1957

"Dance with me," he demanded.

The reception, where I was the center of attention, faded into insignificance. My eyes locked on his dark, compelling face, and I let him lead me onto the dance floor. Moving into his arms was heaven. I couldn't control the tiny sigh of absolute satisfaction as he drew me close enough to feel the beating of his heart. He was a gorgeous man—dark hair, dark liquid eyes and a burning fire in them to possess me.

I knew who he was. I'd heard rumors that he was a prince of Egypt, descended from the pharaohs and that he was a connoisseur of women, which meant he might be the one. The perfect passion that I'd been searching for.

He said he wanted me to join him at his palace. He said he desired me.

We stood in the middle of the floor, bodies melded, hearts thudding as one. Of course, I protested leaving the reception, but he insisted that the festivities could go on without me.

I wanted to experience the forbidden with him,

so I left and soon found myself whisked to his palace on the edge of Cairo.

He brought me into an amazing room that had a bubbling fountain in it along with small divans with numerous pillows.

He wasted no time as he pulled me to him and kissed my lips. He tasted of heady wine and the exotic. My mouth felt sensitized and tingled with each kiss he gave me until I was moaning into his hard kisses.

He took each piece of clothing off as if this were some kind of a dance to him. I loved his rhythm, this humming delight I couldn't contain.

His mouth was hot on my body, my breasts. I cried out when I felt him pour something heavy onto my breast. When I opened my eyes, I saw him smile. He held a jar in his hand and I could see the thick amber liquid was honey. He told me that I was an exquisite flower. I giggled like an idiot. No man had ever said such a thing to me.

Then he dipped his fingers in the honey and brought it to my lips. I thought I would come apart at the seams, as I tasted the sweetness on my tongue. He kissed me, savoring the taste, too, his tongue exploring my mouth. Then he lowered his head and took my nipple into his mouth, sucking at the honey and my flesh.

I writhed beneath him and, still, as he suckled me, he poured the honey over my other breast. A delicious tightness filled my groin at the feel of the amber liquid sliding over my hot, taut nipple. When his tongue caught and followed the slide of the honey to my aching bud, I cried out and climaxed, the sensations exploding inside me like firecrackers.

He took me then, pushing his hard, full heat inside me in one penetrating thrust. Another climax was upon me and I gave myself over to his lovemaking.

Afterward, as I lay sated in his arms, he told me about his ancestors and produced these jewel-encrusted rings. Of course, in my naiveté, I thought they were earrings. But he soon told me that they didn't go into the ears, but attached to the nipples and women wore them as an erotic enticement to their men. I was intrigued by them and asked him how the women went about getting their nipples pierced.

He asked me if I would be interested in wearing them for him. I told him that they excited me and that I wanted to try.

October 12, 1957

The next time we came together, I disrobed for him and danced to the fast-paced Moroccan music coming from his Victrola. When I revealed my breasts, he gasped at the sight of the rings in my nipples. I felt such power over him, his desire clear on his face. The rings swung from my flesh and felt so decadently erotic that I climaxed while I danced.

When the music ended, he pulled me down onto the divan and rasped his tongue over my pierced nipples. It was like no sensation I've ever felt before as I climaxed so hard I could barely catch my breath. Then he was inside me, taking me back up to the heights of passion.

It was only later when he was asleep that I lay in his arms and ached inside. Why? I don't know. It was more and all that I wanted to experience, but I just don't know why I feel this way.

I left Egypt with the rings, the memory of his lovemaking and nothing more.

Jenna lay on the four-poster bed in her room and closed the diary, breathing hard, aching with unfilled desire. Such passion and need taken and enjoyed in abandon. How would it feel to let go? Perhaps that was the lesson of the diary and the passages written in her gran's delicate hand.

The day had passed in a whirlwind of activity. Once the Stantons arrived Jenna abandoned the desk, as she'd gone on to rehearse for some time in the college's beautiful theater. The acoustics were so deliciously right for each note she played.

The reception for students and faculty was a blur of faces, questions and appreciation. She greeted, answered, talked, ate and had a wonderful time. The people in this small town were generous and sweet.

When she'd gotten back to the Wildcatter, Maria was there and Sam had already arrived, as well, but he'd missed dinner because six longhorns had dropped their brood, along with another two mares. It was long past midnight and she'd heard him come in an hour ago. He was probably asleep by now and she would be free to search the desk.

She got up from the bed, tucking the red diary back

into her briefcase. It was time to go find the other diary and that scandalous jewelry. Nipple rings?

Her gran was an adventurous one and it made her suddenly wonder how that would feel.

Jenna slipped out of her room, drawing the diaphanous nightgown around her. She glanced toward Sam's room, the longing inside her more intense than she'd yet felt. Reading her gran's diary always seemed to put her on edge.

She imagined him in that bed, the covers dislodged, the moonlight painting his skin. She leaned against the wall and brought herself under control. Her rampant desires would have to wait.

She descended the stairs quietly and made her way to the office. Twisting the handle, she opened the door. In the dim light she saw the figure of a man sitting in a leather chair with his arm bent, a glint of a glass halfway to his lips.

"Jenna?"

Sam was still up and she was caught. He stood, setting the glass on the table next to the chair. She moved into the room unable to retreat. He stood and she got a glimpse of his face. He seemed different tonight somehow. His eyes were hooded and intense. He looked as if he was in need of relaxation.

It was apparent that he'd just finished showering. His dark hair was damp, curling around his neck and feathering across his forehead. The dark blue chamois shirt that he wore made his eyes shine like lasers and was gaping open, allowing her a tantalizing view of his chest. Her eyes noted his well-worn blue jeans, unbuttoned and loose around his trim waist.

"What are you doing up so late? You must be tired," Jenna said breathlessly, trying to cover up her surprise and her sudden devastating arousal.

"I can't sleep. It's either this or spend my time howling at the moon." He ran a hand through his hair, displacing his shirt so that she caught a glimpse of his muscular ribs.

She swallowed, her mouth suddenly dry. She reached over and snatched his glass of whiskey, needing the distraction. She took too large a swallow and coughed. The whiskey spread like wildfire in her chest and she gasped, dumping the remainder of the liquid down the front of her gown.

Jenna looked at the wet stain. The whiskey dampened a path of silk over one nipple and left a narrow line of shadow all the way to her groin. His eyes tracked the movement of the liquid, watching with narrowed intent the expansion of the whiskey as it was absorbed into the silk of her nightgown.

She blinked rapidly, her eyes tearing from the potent liquid. She wasn't a drinker, and what had possessed her to take such a deep swallow could only be labeled as unease.

She dared to meet Sam's eyes and what she saw there made the glass drop from her nervous fingers. With his chest heaving, he stood, staring at her with a hot gaze burning in his eyes, and desire etched in the very sinew of his muscles. His eyes raked over her body with such a possessive, savage look that she felt a surge of warm, wet desire saturate the soft curls of her femininity. A look that made her tremble, a look that submerged her in sultry need.

His power, his masculine beauty, and his blatant purpose for her captivated Jenna.

Dark blue eyes, hot with a look of stark desire collided with her deep brown ones. She felt that collision throughout her, igniting her passion.

She parted the open shirt and pushed the material off his shoulders. The shirt fell to the carpet. She brushed her fingers along the strong breastbone that defined his torso. Feathering her palms over the hard nub of his nipple, he hissed in a breath. The sound caused little frissons of heat to dance in her stomach, multiply on her skin. With a soft sound, she hesitated, closing her eyes. She wanted him so much, her blood a pounding tempo in her head, but she just had to be clear about what she wanted from him. She was losing the indifference she usually had when she took her pleasure with a man. It frightened her down to her toes.

She trailed her hands across his chest and walked behind him. Pressing against his back, she placed her lips on the corded muscles of his heavy trapezius muscle and kissed his hot skin. With her hands, she molded the taut thickness, skimming her hand down his spine. She turned her head and her hand froze.

The desk stood in the darkness like a crouching giant ready to destroy and conquer. Guilt assaulted her in waves. Seducing Sam to get to the diary made her feel cheap. Anything they had together would be tainted by her duplicity.

Sam turned, took hold of her upper arms and drew her close.

"Do you enjoy torturing me?"

Without waiting for an answer, he pulled the material of her nightgown across her breast and lowered his mouth. The hot, wet, unbearable sensation of his clever mouth made Jenna loose her tentative control. He sucked hard on her nipple and a broken cry came from her as she twisted against his mouth.

She looked up at him and suddenly was overwhelmed by her needs, her emotions. With a sob, she darted away from him and ran from the office.

He caught her halfway up the stairs. "Jenna, shoot, I'm sorry. I thought you were teasing me. I didn't mean to scare you."

She struggled against his hold. His hand dropped of its own accord and traveled quickly to fasten on her waist. She freed herself from his grasp and fled to her room, trying to turn away the out-of-control sensation taking over her body.

She stopped suddenly, stunned at the woman she saw in the full-length cheval mirror. Her face was taut and wild, her eyes deep and sultry. Her mouth was red as a berry, her body lush, her nipples beaded against the black silk of her gown. Through the dim light from the hall she could see the outline of her body.

Sam came up behind her. He groaned softly when he saw what she saw. She watched him in the reflection of the mirror. His mouth went to her throat, his lips burned her skin. Her gaze was momentarily cut off as her eyes closed and a shivery sensation cascaded like warm rain along her heated body.

Her eyes flew open when she felt his hands in her hair. Slowly, seductively she watched his rapt face, lingering on the hard-chiseled mouth and strongly arrogant jaw as he removed the elastic that held her hair in a braid. The simple unraveling of her hair had changed into a provocative act. Her shimmering hair came free in a wild, tumbling mass around her shoulders.

Sam lowered the narrow straps of her gown down her slim arms and dipped his head to kiss the exposed skin of her back. The thin material slid down to her wrists. When he raised his head again, she wiggled from the narrow straps, her hands reaching back to cup his head. Twisting her face to him, she sought his mouth.

He pulled her even closer, lowered his mouth and met hers. Her lips were hot, wet, tangy with the flavor of the whiskey. It wasn't whiskey that caused this heady feeling, this intoxicating passion.

With his mouth still firmly on her enticing lips, he lifted her up to his ravenous kiss. He slanted his mouth across hers for a better, more satisfying angle. His tongue skimmed over hers and then captured it.

Releasing her mouth, he saw that the damp fabric had caught on one of her taut nipples and he groaned softly as he reached up and freed the silk. Her pouting nipple thrust against his fingers as Jenna cried out, arching her back into his chest. With a tug, he set the material free. His eyes watched in the mirror at the sensuous glide of the silky fabric as it slipped down her body to pool on the floor around her feet. He watched his face contort into an agony of pleasure as he fought for mastery over his highly aroused body. He waited for the heated, electrifying rush to ease.

She had on nothing but a tiny piece of silk, obscuring her lusciousness from him.

He thrust his hips against her buttocks sliding his hands up over her hips to her sleek belly, trailing his fingertips over her ribs. Jenna moved feverishly against him.

His mouth went to her shoulder, sliding his tongue along her sweet skin to her neck at the same time he cupped her pretty, shapely breasts, her tight pink nipples drawn to firm points against the palms of his hands.

Sam raised his head slightly and looked into the mirror with narrowed eyes. It was obvious to him that Jenna was beyond herself, lost in the drugging sensation of his hands, and a powerful need drove through him. Sparks danced inside him at the smooth, full feel of her breasts in his hands. His breath caught at the sharp sensation, so powerful it made him ache.

He slid his hand down until he found the core of her, hidden from him. He rubbed his thumb rhythmically against the nerve-rich nub. Jenna cried out and he sighed with satisfaction as she bucked hard against him.

Jenna turned toward him, her hands sliding down his chest to the waistband. With sure, tantalizing movements, she pressed the heel of her hand against the hard, long length straining against his fly. The pulsating hardness in his groin nearly exploded when she slipped her fingers beneath the waistband. He ground his mouth hungrily against hers, heat searing through him as she lightly smoothed her thumb over the moist, slick tip of his arousal.

Sam clenched his teeth at the feel of her hands closing around his throbbing erection. His control shredded when she stroked his pulsating flesh in her hands. Sam's face contorted at the sharp, intense pleasure that ricocheted through him. An impatient moment later, the jeans were pushed off his hips and she was cradling all of him between her hands.

With an uncontrollable need he pressed into her hands, closing his eyes as she cupped him, giving him intense and mind-shattering pleasure.

He pulled out of her grasp, turning her until her back was against his chest once again. Sliding his hand beneath the thin elastic of the thong, he drew the silky garment down her legs.

He lifted her body and kicked the scrap of cloth out of the way. Setting her back on her feet, he knelt down. Dragging his chest over her buttocks and sliding his hand along her back, he urged her forward. He found her sex hot, wet against his mouth. He pleasured her with his tongue. He eased a finger inside her and soft whimpers filled his ears like music.

She moaned and her inner muscles clenched. He used his hand on her inner thigh to widen her stance, and his other arm snaked around her stomach pulling her closer. He took her in a deep, wild kiss, at the same time probing more deeply with his finger. His tongue rubbed rhythmically in accompaniment to his finger. Jenna cried out again and again at the double onslaught.

He wanted her to remember him, drown out any other encounter she'd ever had until he was the only man who could make her this hot, this wild. The sound of her pleasure shattered his own control. He wanted her. Now. Right now. He didn't want to wait, couldn't take a few precious moments to move her to a bed. He rose in one fluid movement. Shoving his jeans and briefs off completely, he quickly tossed them aside. Reaching for her again, he bent her at the waist. Grasping her hips, he thrust forward, the tip of his cock pushing just against her tight core. With his eyes squeezed tightly together, he threw back his head and clenched his teeth. His body was full to overflowing, his muscles shaking as he fought the ever-growing ache.

"Please, Sam," she pleaded. She moved feverishly against him, groaning.

"What about protection?"

"It's okay. Sam, please."

With a powerful thrust he plunged into her, driving his hips in one long, strong slide.

Gaining a moment's control, Sam stopped moving. Sweat beading on his brow and sliding down his chest, with formidable effort he held himself in check. An agony of sensation shot through him when she flexed her hips, her hot, wet tightness gripping him, stroking him, drawing him to culmination.

His next thrust was deeper, and Jenna cried out brokenly, her tight muscles gripping his shaft. She moved against him frantically, accepting his thrust. His hips slammed against her buttocks, and suddenly she stiffened and groaned deeply, her delicate movements clasping him like a glove. It was all it took to shatter Sam's control. With one harder, deeper thrust, the swelling need crested and claimed him.

8

IT TOOK A LONG TIME before either of them was aware of their position or could speak coherently. Sam gently stepped away from her as Jenna straightened and turned to twine her arms around his neck, one hand entangling in the longer hair at his nape. The way they had lost control was amazing to her. Her previous encounters had been tame compared to this. But the strength of her desire erased the single moment of panic she'd had in the office. Why was she running from what she wanted?

This was how she wanted Sam, unleashing the sizzling passion she detected in his eyes. Their flirting dance of desire, from the moment she met him at the airport, had led her to this—the most amazing sexual experience of her life.

Sam stared at her and reached up a hand to brush away the damp hair against her cheek. Tears stung her eyes at the tender way he touched her as he slipped his arms around her and held her close. With a movement that was as easy as opening a door, he scooped her up and, ignoring the clothes haphazardly strewn behind them, took her to his room. He knelt on the bed and laid her carefully down. She didn't let go of his shoulders.

He studied her face in the moonlight. After several long seconds he spoke. "Stay with me tonight." His voice was low. She pulled him closer to her, unable to let him go. Cupping his jaw, the scratchy feel of his beard rasped against her palm, another sensual goad to her tingling body.

She closed her eyes tightly for a moment. An emotion washed over her that she couldn't identify, didn't dare identify. He wanted her to stay. Sleep with him, something she'd never done in the past. It seemed too intimate, too trusting. She'd never been needed like this before and the feeling caused gut-wrenching fear.

He pulled her into his arms and she snuggled close to him, pushing the fear aside. For the first time in her life, that awful ugly feeling of loneliness didn't weigh heavily on her heart.

This was temporary, she told herself as she sighed against the warmth of Sam's arms. Only temporary.

JENNA AWOKE at the feel of Sam's hot mouth on her breast. She turned to him, burying her hand in his hair, dragging her palm over his shoulder. He pulled powerfully at her breast, pushing her back slightly so that he could get to her other aching nipple. "Sam," she said fiercely as he bit her, making her think of the exquisite pleasure and pain of nipple rings. A hard stab of sensation drove into her core as she thrust upward toward Sam, seeking the hardness of his body to alleviate the ache of hers.

Her hand trailed over his hip, her fingers pressing rhythmically into his flesh. She caressed his muscled thighs, skirted his straining erection and stroked his belly. He moaned against her breast, his hands going to the button of nerves between her legs. She cried out as he stroked her and entered her with his finger. She trailed her fingers downward again, closer this time but still avoiding his hard length.

Finally, he groaned. "Touch me," he begged huskily. "C'mon, sugar, you're driving me crazy."

"Bite me again, Sam. It feels so good." He complied, taking her nipple and rolling it against his teeth. She curled her hand around his cock and jerked her hand up and down. Sam jackknifed against her. She pushed at him and rolled him onto his back, enjoying the way he couldn't stop flexing his hips, driving his erection against the hand she'd wrapped around him. When her mouth covered the head of his penis, he bucked and cried out her name. The skin was so silky and hot she explored the round tip with her tongue. Sam thrust uncontrollably against her mouth as she took all of him, sucking hard, pulling his hips off the bed with each long movement of her mouth.

He grabbed her shoulders and dragged her up his body. "Jen, please," he begged, and she eased down on him slowly. He twisted his head and she came up and then teased him again with just a few more inches. "Damn, Jen, you're killing me."

She absorbed another inch of him and then another. Her thighs were trembling from the aching torture. She wanted him as much as he wanted her.

"Jen," he pleaded now, thrusting his hips upward, and she drove herself to the hilt. He cried out and captured her mouth in a deep, wet kiss that spoke of his need. One hand went to her bottom, pressing her more firmly against him, and she squirmed beneath his touch, wanting to be even closer. He stroked a finger between her legs and she bucked against him at the touch.

He surged upward, and her gasp became a cry. The rhythm of his thrusts were wildly intoxicating, driving him deeper and deeper within her. Jenna gave herself up to the need rocketing through her. Her knees clasped his hips tighter and tighter, until the ultimate explosion wrung a cry from her lips. She fell forward, and he lifted her one more time until he was moaning with his own release.

She made a murmur of protest when he rolled her off him, but soon quieted when he pulled her into his arms.

THE NEXT TIME Jenna opened her eyes, she encountered a sleeping Sam. His eyes were closed, his chest heaving evenly. She sighed while she looked at him, feeling tender emotions curl around her heart.

Sam filled her vision. He lay on his back, his dark hair like ink against the stark whiteness of the pillow, one arm thrown over his head and the other flung straight out in her direction, as if in supplication, so close to her that she could reach out and touch him.

If she could only touch him, everything would be okay. Sunlight from a break in the blinds crossed his hand and bare forearm. The sun turned his dark skin almost…golden.

She pushed herself up on her elbow, and in slow increments she reached toward his extended hand. His palm lay upturned and half-open, the fingers curled in soft relaxation. His hands were big, the fingers long and blunt. They looked like working man's hands—tough and capable. Her eyes traveled up from his palm to his wrist, where the pulse beat slowly underneath the smooth skin. She longed to touch such vibrant life. Life that pulsed from him with radiant promise and languid heat.

She had defined herself one specific way for all of her life. She'd kept her relationships casual and temporary. In her meaningless encounters, she'd chosen unavailable men. Men who wouldn't be interested in committing. Men who wouldn't tie her down. Men who wouldn't get hurt by her own inability to commit. If they didn't love her, she couldn't hurt them.

She licked her lips, wanting so much just to touch him. The sheet had slipped off his shoulder and arm; his biceps, even in sleep, was taut with a velvet swell of bare skin and muscle.

She imagined smoothing her palm across his shoulder. Her heart beat faster. She could see the outline of his body beneath the sheet, the fluent shape of his torso and hip, powerful, relaxed perfection, his leg drawn up a little for comfort.

There was an ache in her, a restlessness. She was on the edge of something she wanted and could not have.

Her hand closed in midair just inches from his and then she drew back.

The shock of his warm hand clasping hers made her eyes flash to his face. He'd turned his head and had been watching her.

He smiled, tugged, and Jenna was enticed forward

onto his chest, straddling his body until she was as close to him as she could get.

He gave her an amused look, the creases around his eyes crinkling, the intimate glimmer setting off sensations in her midriff that made her pulse skip and falter. He held her gaze, an almost smile in his eyes, and then he gently reached out and grabbed a thick strand of her hair, absently rubbing it between his fingers. He tugged gently. "Morning."

"It is that."

"It was one hell of a night."

"Yes, it was that, too."

"Are you always so amicable in the morning?"

"Only when I'm fully satisfied and wholly ravished."

His eyebrows rose. Watching him stretched out like a big dangerous cat, with his intense blue eyes, tangled lashes and faint, lazy smile brought back vivid memories of how she'd been thoroughly enticed.

"Ravished. I like that."

"Mmm…so did I." Jenna shifted restlessly against Sam's hips. Last night had been wonderful and Jenna's thoughts returned to her gran's diary. Her gran had been on a journey for what seemed like a long time to find what Jenna hadn't even been looking for—mind-numbing, body-crushing passion. She looked down into Sam's sleepy, dreamy eyes and tried to gain control over her shaken emotions.

Feeling a pang of guilt, she looked away from him, her gaze landing on the pocket watch that Sam must have put on his nightstand. She braced her hand against the bed and reached over, scooping up the watch. Positioning herself against Sam's chest by folding her elbows and leaning forward, she examined the outside.

"It was my great-grandfather's. He gave it to my grandfather, who gave it to my dad. When my dad died…" Sam's words trailed off, and the pain in his voice drew her eyes to his face. She could see the grief, the loss, and both went straight to her heart. How could she not believe that this man who had such a sentimental attachment to a piece of his history wouldn't understand about her quest to get the diary back and keep them both from prying eyes?

She slipped her arms around his neck, pressing her breasts flat against his chest. For a silent moment, she held him. Her own loss welled up in her chest. "Tell me."

"It was part of what he bequeathed to me. The ranch, the livestock, all of it. If there had been a more modern hospital, my dad might have survived the heart attack."

"So that is why you're so dedicated to the renovation of the hospital?"

"That, and to help the people in the surrounding area. It's what my father would have wanted. Not for himself, mind you, but for the people of Savannah. People my great-grandmother loved. Even now, we're still a tight-knit community although we've grown some."

"That's something to cherish, Sam."

"I do cherish it. I feel as if I have a responsibility to these people passed down from my great-grandfather. He built this ranch and the town with his own blood, sweat and tears.'' He pressed on the time-piece and the face popped open.

''I can understand why you feel responsible for the legacy that your father left you. My legacy is music. My gran was a famous opera singer in her time. My mother followed in her footsteps.''

''Why did you choose the violin then?''

''I didn't want to compete with my mother.''

''Why not?''

''My gran raised me because my mother was too busy with her career. Opera is her life. She needs it—the fame, the adulation. She wouldn't appreciate me taking the spotlight away from her.''

''Are you good?''

''Vocally?''

He smiled and ran his hand up her hip. ''Shoot, yeah. What did you think I meant?''

She flashed him a cheeky smile and said, ''My gran said I could have had a career in the opera. Whether I would have climbed to a higher pinnacle than my mother, I couldn't say. But the violin is what I love.''

''You say that as if it's the only thing you love.''

''Since my gran died, it is, Sam.''

He nodded. ''No room for anything else?''

''No.''

He looked away from her, shifting to the edge of the bed. He closed the timepiece and placed the watch on the nightstand.

When he turned back to her, he cupped her face. ''That's sad, Jenna. Real sad.''

''My mother wasn't around. I retreated into my

music for solace. I'm a self-sufficient, independent woman, and I like my life that way. I don't think it's sad."

"You don't see any future for yourself."

"Sure I do. I hope to teach at a prestigious college someday or open my own school."

"I mean a family, Jenna."

Her stomach jumped. "Never. I can't see myself being a mother."

"Because your own was so distant?"

"I don't think I can dedicate myself to a family and to my music. I'm not willing to give it up like my gran did."

He pulled her close and held her. "That's too bad."

She leaned against him and agreed with him. It was too bad, but it was the way it had to be. The thought of people depending on her, expecting something from her, frightened her.

After a moment, Sam said, "How about a trip into town? You need those duds if you're going to take a tour of the ranch with me."

Guilt assaulted her deep in her gut. He'd been so kind and had even gotten over having her in his home. Yet she was still hiding her real reason for being here. She would tell him the truth, and, at least in that respect, deal with him on an honest basis.

"Sam?"

"Mmm," he mumbled as he buried his face in her neck, sending goose bumps down her arms and peaking her naked nipples into hard buds.

"I would like to tell you…" The shrill ringing of

the phone made Jenna jump, and Sam automatically reached for the intrusive instrument.

"Winchester."

He listened for a few minutes. A frown appeared on his face. "We're short? By how much?"

Jenna watched him focus on the conversation and she slid to the edge of the bed, looking for her nightgown, and then remembered it'd been left behind at her mirror.

"Don't worry, Lester. We'll get the extra we need. I'll talk to the contractors." He paused and his voice got firmer. "I'll get it any way I can. I'd even sell my soul. That's a promise. The renovation of the hospital is my number one priority."

Hopeless regret crept through her at his words, causing a zinging, jagged pain in her heart. She closed her eyes, realizing how close she'd come to exposing her secret, exposing her gran's private, erotic thoughts to people who wouldn't understand, nor appreciate a young girl's search for passion.

Although she sensed that Sam was a good man, and nothing like her uncle or the judge, Sam's altruistic motives were obvious and stated. He'd be susceptible to exploiting her grandmother's treasure. Jenna wanted to trust him, but she couldn't risk her gran's diary for something that could prove too fragile to survive Sam's dedication to a very deserving cause.

What she and Sam shared wasn't strong and enduring. It was just sex—great sex—but sex nonetheless. After four days in Sam's presence, it was clear to her that he followed through on all matters that were important to him. She would have to put her physical reaction to Sam in perspective and carry on with her own agenda.

Get the diary and get out.

Sam smiled at her from the other side of the bed. "So, what were you going to say?"

"That it'll only take me forty-five minutes to get ready to go into town."

She left Sam's room and hastily showered and dressed, but when she opened her door, she realized that Sam wasn't ready yet. She closed the door, taking a deep breath. Walking over to the bed, she bent down, opened her briefcase and pulled out her grandmother's diary.

November 20, 1957

Her name was Madam Bridgett Delacroix. After she saw my performance, she invited me to come to her estate and stay overnight. I was thrilled because, after several days of practices and performances, I wanted to see something of France before I left.

When we got to her estate, lunch was served on her patio in view of the magnificent gardens.

While we were eating, a gorgeous man came over to the table. He had dark eyes and hair. When he was introduced to me, he kissed my hand, lingering over my fingers. It sent goose bumps up and down my arm. She introduced him as her good friend Henri and, soon after, took my hand and led me into the house.

I could feel his intense eyes on me as I walked

away. I really wanted to stay in the garden and talk to him, but my manners are impeccable and I couldn't be rude to my hostess.

There were erotic paintings on the walls and scandalous sculpture decorating her shelves and tables. I tried not to look, but the art fascinated me. She saw my interest and indicated that I should look at whatever I liked.

I asked her where she had gotten all her art. She smiled with a secret light in her eye and told me here and there.

November 21, 1957

The next morning, when I went downstairs, I found her in the living room. She was just closing my diary. I realized that I left it downstairs the night before. I took it out of her hands, telling her that it was private. I was very upset.

She was intrigued with my journey and told me that she was a courtesan. She said that as a lady, she reserved her time for a select few. She was always attentive, personable and responsive. She said her services were available to affluent gentlemen who desire to experience the ultimate in first-class companionship.

She took my hand and led me upstairs to her room. There she went to her jewelry box. She pulled out a fine gold chain and put it in my hands.

She told me to wear the chain under my clothes and it would make me feel sexy and powerful.

She told me that Henri was very interested in me

and if I was interested in continuing my journey, she was sure he would oblige me.

I agreed and she told me to go to my room. I did and disrobed, draping the fine chain around my waist.

When I heard the knock on the door, I told him to come in. He came up to me. His warm hands caressed my waist, making my skin tingle as he circled my whole body. He told me I was beautiful and released the pins in my hair. The feel of it cascading over my shoulders and down my back was a sensual goad. I moaned softly when he moved the heavy mass of my hair and softly kissed the back of my neck. His lips were soft, heavenly. He toyed with the chain at my waist and I felt the desire in my belly increase with each featherlight touch of his fingers. His hands moved up my body, cupping my bare breasts.

"Please" was all I could whisper and he kneaded my flesh. I feverishly wanted his hot palms against my sensitive nipples.

He groaned as he moved around to the front of me, taking my mouth in a burning kiss that ignited my blood. Then his mouth moved down to my nipples and he sucked and bit them until I couldn't breathe. His mouth moved lower, his tongue stroking my skin. When he came back to my mouth, I reached for his belt and unfastened his pants, pushing the offensive garments off him.

The hardness of his erection filled my hands. He looked deep into my eyes. He asked me if I knew how to pleasure a man with my mouth. I hadn't ever tried it, but I wanted to.

He led me to the bed and sat down, drawing me between his thighs and tugging me into a kneeling position. I lowered my mouth to take him. He groaned and thrust against my lips and then he was inside. I had no idea that a woman had such power over a man. He told me what to do. Oh, his words were wicked, wild and wonderful. I made him writhe and saw his hands clench in the coverlet. It was heady and wonderful.

Finally he couldn't take any more. He dragged me onto the mattress and told me that it was now my turn to be pleasured. When his mouth touched my sex, I cried out with shocked pleasure. Again, I had no idea.

Finally he surged up my heated body and plunged himself inside me with a force that made me arch and cry out.

He was big and hard, with a fullness that made me twist beneath him. It was thrilling and passionate, beyond my imagination to conjure.

Afterward, I left in the car I'd come in, carrying another souvenir to add to my growing collection of erotic jewelry. A tangible object to remember the passion I shared in a beautiful estate in Paris. A passion that was wonderful yet still unfulfilling. My journey would have to continue.

Jenna placed the diary back into her briefcase. She closed her eyes, wondering how any other man could possibly have been better in bed than Sam. Even now, standing here, she wanted him again.

Without hesitating, she left the room and made her way back to Sam's. She shed her clothes and opened his bathroom door.

He leaned into her when she stepped into the shower, her hands slipping around his waist, her body pressing up against the hard muscles of his back. "Do you mind if it takes an hour for me to get ready?"

Sam turned around and laughed softly as he took her mouth.

JENNA IMAGINED that Savannah would be a one-street town with a stoplight, a grocery store, bank, diner and town hall. There was a town hall, but the town had more than just one bank. There were several and, although there was a diner, there were also many eating establishments they passed on their way to Kellar Mercantile. They stopped in front of the redbrick store and Sam ushered her inside.

"Hi there, Sam," a young woman said as she approached them. "This here that pretty musician I've heard so much about?"

"She's the one. Knocked the socks off the high-rollers from Houston and Galveston the other night with her fine performance."

The woman stuck out her hand. "Pleased to meet you. I'm Lurlene Kellar. My father and mother own the store. We're so happy that you were kind enough to volunteer to help us out. My ma isn't as well as she'd like us to believe and the new hospital makes me feel a lot better about her getting the proper care she needs.''

A new, unexpected concern gripped Jenna. She hadn't considered these people when she'd volunteered her services or what the new hospital would mean to them. She was from New York where emergency help could be called in the blink of an eye. She'd never worried about getting health care. But these people were dependent on the one hospital close to their town, and for the first time in Jenna's life she felt as if her music made a material difference. Instead of playing for the intense enjoyment of people, she was actually making a contribution to better these people's lives.

Jenna took Lurlene's hand and squeezed in genuine pleasure. ''Thank you for being so kind.''

''It's not kindness but the dang truth.''

''Lurlene—'' her mother looked up from ringing up a customer ''—you watch your language.'' She nodded and smiled at Jenna and Sam before returning her attention to the customer.

Lurlene looked chagrined and Sam didn't help any when he laughed and nudged her. The young girl pushed him back and snickered.

The easy way these people had with each other suddenly made her envious. She always shopped in the same stores in New York, but not one of the salesladies knew her by name.

''What can I show you today?''

''This little lady needs the works—jeans, boots and shirts. She only packed city clothes.'' Sam rolled his eyes.

"Well, you came to the right place. Let me show you what we have."

Going up and down the aisles, Lurlene started to pile jeans and shirts onto Sam's outstretched arms until she reached the boot section of the store.

Jenna looked at all the gleaming leather, then down at Sam's boots. It hit home that his sturdy, battered boots with a good-size heel had seen more wear and tear than her shoes ever would. Sam was a one-hundred-percent, dyed-in-the-wool cowboy and she had the privilege of seeing him work his ranch.

Lurlene left them at the dressing room and went back to the front of the store.

Jenna changed quickly and stepped out of the dressing room, watching Sam's eyes light up as she faced him. "Sam, what do you think of these jeans?"

Sam swallowed. He knew she had a tight little figure because he'd seen her naked, but there was something stirring about a woman in a pair of jeans that molded and cupped every beautiful inch of her body. It was enough to make a man sweat. "They look painted on, but there's not a damn thing wrong with that." He stood up and walked over to her, glancing over his shoulder to check where Lurlene was. When he spied her helping another customer, he backed Jenna into the shadow of the dressing room doorway.

"But let me check the fit." He slid his hands over her buttocks while Jenna buried her face in his shirt and tried to muffle her laughter.

"You are incorrigible, Sam Winchester."

She looked up at him and he smiled at the glint in her eyes. A jolt to his heart made him move closer to her. He suddenly felt he couldn't get as close as he wanted to.

"How about some lunch? You kept me too preoccupied this morning for breakfast," she groused.

"Perish the thought of you not being able to fill out these jeans to perfection," he said, squeezing her butt and letting her go. "I just have to stop at the Levoie Steel and Leather Works to pick up a new set of roping spurs."

"Roping spurs?"

She looked up at him with the most adorable confusion on her face. So different from the way she'd looked last night. She'd been light and fire in his arms; burning him, melting him until he couldn't think, only react. He remembered her soft skin, her harsh cries, the feel of her rapture and the satisfaction he felt because she was beneath his hands, his body, in his bed where he'd wanted her from the start.

He shouldn't have, but he did. He told himself this was a temporary affair. She didn't belong here with him. She belonged on stages in cities around the world—places he'd only read about.

"Let's pay for this stuff and I'll show you what I mean."

It took no time at all to cash out and walk the short distance to Levoie's.

Sam went up to the counter and rang the bell. A large man came from the back and smiled. He pulled a box out from under the counter. "Here you go, Sam. Just what you ordered. I finished them yesterday."

Sam opened the box and pulled out the steel spurs with the leather buckles. "Fine craftsmanship as usual, Tiny." He turned to Jenna. "Roping spurs are used to control a horse when a cowboy is roping cattle," he said, showing her the pair. "There is no tie-down under the heel like there is for rodeo spurs."

"That makes sense. I guess I didn't realize that there were different spurs for different jobs. I just like the way they jingle when you walk."

"You do?"

"Sure, it's such a sexy sound. Come to think of it. I like the way you walk. Purposeful, solid, like you know where you're going and what you have to do. Not to mention *your* cute butt in the tight jeans you wear."

He rolled his shoulders at her compliment, trying to tamp down the sheer undiluted pleasure he got from her words. "The jingling is caused by jingle bobs and that's the only reason they're on the spurs."

"Hey, Tiny, show Jenna a pair of regular spurs."

She took the spurs that Tiny gave her. "These little teardrop-shaped thingies?"

"Yeah," he said, smiling when she made the rowel spin. "Are you ready to go?"

"Sure, but don't I need a hat?"

"You sure do and I know exactly the right one. He walked over to the ladies hats and chose a black Mexican-style hat with little conchos around the brim. When she walked over he set it on her head. "Come on, cowgirl, let's get something to fill your belly."

9

SAM SHIFTED in his seat, his eyes glued to the computer's flat screen. Ensconced in an overstuffed chair in his disassembled office with the laptop on his lap, he tried to concentrate on the column of figures in front of him, but his mind just simply wandered.

The morning had dawned bright and clear, and even though it had been almost a week that Jenna had been on his ranch, he knew that soon their time would run out. She would go home and he would get on without her.

He'd left her in his bed, sleeping off another night of lovemaking. Although he hadn't had much sleep, he felt invigorated and decided to do his chores early. With time to spare, he'd come to his office to tackle the books.

She'd been a revelation last night, a miracle. She'd been incredible in his hands, her skin so soft he'd wanted to lay his head against it and dream, her eyes so deep and sweet that he'd drunk from them like a well. As he pitched bales of hay to the pastured horses, he thought of the dance of her body in the shadows. As he filled troughs he remembered the song of passion on her lips. As he trudged through mud and grass, he was warmed by the memories of her candor, her spirit, her hunger.

And Tooter had never been as hostile about Tiffany, even as he'd warned Sam about her highfalutin ways. Did Tooter see a more immediate threat in Jenna? And, if he did, what did that mean to Sam's heart? Tiffany had barely grazed the surface. But Jenna, she was deep under his skin. A fever that heated and infected his blood.

Ten minutes later, swearing softly, Sam clicked on all the appropriate icons to shut down the computer. He wouldn't get anything done anyway. The thought of the way he had left Jenna this morning filled his senses. Her exposed shoulders, the spill of her coffee-colored hair on his pillow, and the silhouette of her smooth curvy body filled his mind. He wondered if she was still asleep.

The sound of the opening door drew Sam's eyes. But where he expected to see Maria ready with her dusting supplies, he saw only the delicate features of Jenna. Her slim body was decked out in her new jeans and red-and-gold-plaid shirt. He swallowed hard when he saw her bare feet and her sexy painted toenails.

She moved across the floor toward the back of his office. In the dim light, he was sure she didn't see him. She stopped in front of his prized Remington sculpture of a cowboy and bucking bronc that his great-grandfather had gotten for a song before the sculptor had become a legend. Gently, she ran her hands over the sculpture and he wondered what thoughts were going through her head. She turned away from it and he saw that she was looking straight at his new desk. When she started in that direction, the noise from the laptop, as it closed down, startled her. She whirled around and met his eyes.

She went rigid and her eyes widened in alarm. True alarm and every Ranger instinct in him went on full alert. She's up to something, the cool rational cop part of his mind told him. He set the laptop on the small table near the armchair and rose. The male part of him wanted to crush her to him and ignore his gut instinct.

"Jenna, what's going on?"

She stared up at him and he felt himself melt inside, but if she were up to something, he would have to shore up his resolve. He grabbed her by her upper arms. "I asked you a question."

"I'm sorry. It's such poor manners. I'm fascinated with you, with everything about you. Your office was too tempting for me to resist."

She placed her hand on his chest and the warmth from her palm started his heart beating hard. His eyes narrowed, not sure whether he was being foolish or if he really did see guilt and alarm cross her face, rather than simple embarrassment.

"Is that so?"

"Yes. The sculpture, the Ranger memorabilia and your antiques say so much about you."

"And that would be?"

"You care about your past and your ancestors. Family is important to you. That draws me to you because it reminds me of my gran. It reminds me how she would hold dear those things that identify us as a family. The old photographs and the new. The things she chose to surround herself with defined her as nostalgic and sweet."

Tears gathered in her eyes. With that, his suspicions diminished and his heart twisted. He quite literally couldn't stand a woman's tears. But Jenna's overwhelmed him, brought all his tender emotions to the surface, brought him to his knees. Her grief was clear in her brown eyes and he remembered how she had comforted him yesterday morning when he'd become all soft about his father's passing. He felt so small that his suspicions were precluding his offering her the same comfort.

He pulled her against his chest, wrapping his arms around her. "Jenna, I'm sorry. I'm just cranky because I had to be cooped up in this office with figures and boring paperwork."

She reached up and touched his face and he leaned into her hand. "Why don't we get out of here for a while?" he suggested.

"I have to practice."

"Later then?"

She nodded.

"How about a tour of the ranch from horseback?"

"I've never ridden before."

"Then it'll be an interesting experience. I guess I'll get back to these numbers and after you're finished practicing, put on your boots and hat and meet me at the corral?"

"Okay."

"ARE YOU PLUMB CRAZY?"

Sam put his hands on his hips and faced down his

foreman. The little man straightened to his full height, bristling with outrage as he continued. ''She's been nothing but a distraction since she got here. Dawson's coming by with those mares he wants serviced. We have foals and calves dropping all over the ranch, yearlings to round up, brush to clear, fences to mend and a herd to move to spring pasture. Does it sound like you have time to lollygag with this woman?''

''Tooter,'' Sam said, his voice full of authority. ''It's just a morning ride. I'll be back and we can get to some of those chores after lunch. You'll have my undivided attention.''

Tooter snatched off his beaten-up Stetson and slapped it against his leg. ''Shoot, boy. I haven't had your undivided attention since that female hit this outfit and you know it.''

''Tooter, I'm not arguing with you. Get Silver Shadow and Black Spot out of their stalls and have them saddled and bridled for me.''

''What? Shadow and Black Spot? They're your mounts.''

''That's right.''

''You goin' to let that city slicker gal ride one of your string?''

''Tooter, I don't think I'm stuttering and I know you're hearing's just fine.''

''It plumb amazes me that you'd let some woman ride one of your personal horses. Tiffany never got close.''

''We're not debating this, Tooter.'' The stubborn old man was bent on saving him from himself and

Sam found it touching but thoroughly irritating. "Tiffany didn't understand horses."

"And this one does?"

"I don't know how to say this, but Jenna's more open to new experiences. Tiffany didn't want to understand horses. She only cared about the image of a cowboy."

"That gal has you knotted up inside if you think she cares about you and this ranch. She isn't going to stay here and be your perfect little ranch gal. She's got better things to do."

Sam spun around to Tooter, but the little man wouldn't back down. Sam knew he was right, but it hurt anyway. Jenna wouldn't stay. Not that he thought she would. Shoot, he wasn't thinking along those terms. He wasn't even trying to convince himself. He and Jenna had sex and exploration going on. That was all. She was curious about him and who he was because he was so different from the men in New York. He was aware that she was as caught up in the image of a cowboy as Tiffany was, but with Jenna, she looked beneath the surface and saw the things that were important to him. That interlude in the office had shaken him. She'd been very close to him then and he'd liked that intimacy, hungered for more of it. But he would have to tamp down that hankering, because Tooter was too damned right.

"Don't you think I know that? I'm not a fool."

"Then stop actin' like one," Tooter said as he turned away, but not before Sam saw the contrite glint in his eye.

JENNA KNEW they were fighting over her. She stood on the front porch as bits and pieces of their conversation floated up to her. When Sam went into the back door of the house, Jenna skirted him and went around the front and followed Tooter into the barn.

The guilt and shame had burned in her as she'd stood in the office and had lied to Sam. But the problem was it wasn't entirely a lie. She was fascinated with him. With everything about him. It was disturbing how she needed to feel his skin against her now when she slept and how first thing in the morning all she cared about were those sleepy, sexy eyes and his strong hands. When she'd woken up this morning, she'd been upset that he'd left, but she thought he had dressed and gone to do his chores. After all, it was a Monday and a workday for him. He'd indulged her all day yesterday. She couldn't expect him to do that every day.

That's why she'd headed to the office early, before anyone else would be around. But he'd been sitting in the shadows with his Wild West look and his laptop. The thought of the diary had been secondary to the beauty of him. The suspicious look in his eyes had alarmed her for reasons she just couldn't seem to name. Reasons she didn't want to explore because it would be too dangerous. To her, but more importantly, to him.

She could hear Tooter cussing and fussing about their fight and it hurt to know she was a bone of contention between them.

Tooter was moving around a big gray horse, slipping a bridle over the animal's nose when she cleared her throat.

He looked over at her, his eyes narrowing.

Jenna was never one to beat around the bush when she had something to say. "All you said about me isn't quite true."

"But some of it is."

"Yes. I'm not staying here. My life is somewhere else. It's only temporary, Tooter. You'll have Sam back soon."

He stepped away from the horse. "You think so? You think Sam is thinking temporary? I know that boy and you're dangerous to him." He pointed his finger at her.

She set her hands on her hips. "I'll be gone soon. Please stop sniping at him. If you have to take your anger out on someone, take it out on me. He's been nothing but a gracious host and kind man."

Tooter eyed her slowly. "Maybe you do care a mite, but not enough."

"Don't judge me."

Tooter turned away and picked up a saddle. "Make sure he understands."

"I promise you that I won't hurt him."

She pretended not to hear him as he mumbled, "Yeah, I bet you will, but Sam is a stubborn feller."

She walked right into Sam as she exited the barn. "I was looking for you," she said before Sam could speculate why she was there.

He looked down at her and smiled. "I was looking for you, too."

The clop of horses' hooves could be heard in the

deep recesses of the barn. "It sounds like Tooter's got those horses saddled."

Jenna looked up at him and couldn't help the tender feelings she had for him. She had to haul back on them, because she'd promised Tooter that she was here only as a guest. And she always kept her promises. She wouldn't hurt Sam. She couldn't bear that. Being like her mother was not an option. Making it clear to him at every turn that she was only here on a day pass would ensure that they would part on amicable terms. There wasn't any reason for Sam to discover why she was really here. She'd get the diary and jewelry and leave without him being the wiser.

"I guess you'd better teach me to ride. Time is growing short and I'll be gone by the end of the week."

Sam's mouth tightened. He forced a smile and nodded. He let her go as Tooter emerged from the barn.

Sam took the reins from the sullen old man and Tooter stomped away.

Sam watched him go and it hurt her to see the pain in his eyes. It was obvious to her that Sam was very fond of the cantankerous foreman. Jenna hoped that Tooter would cool off and he and Sam could be best friends again.

Sam turned to her and dropped the reins of the big gray horse. "Stand," he said softly, and the animal's ears tipped up to catch the command.

He rubbed at the forehead of the next animal, whose coat was black until about the stomach area where there was a smattering of white gradually spreading to the horse's hindquarters that were dotted with black. "This is Black Spot. He's an Appaloosa and one of the smartest, gentlest animals on this ranch."

She could see the pride in Sam. He reached down and snagged her wrist, bringing it toward the horse's nose. "Let him get to know you."

The curious animal stretched out his neck and sniffed at her.

"Rub his forehead gently. He loves that."

She did and he closed his eyes in pleasure. She moved down to his nose and exclaimed a little too loudly, "His nose is so soft." Black Spot sidestepped nervously and eyed her.

"I'm sorry, pretty boy," she crooned, and he settled down, snuffling at the hand she offered. She was thoroughly charmed. "I could get to really like this."

"Wait until you ride him. First you need to tighten the cinch before you mount him."

He moved around to the left of the animal and pointed at the belt that was snug around the horse's stomach. "Unbuckle it and pull it tighter." Jenna did as she was told. Sam came over and said, "Take it up another notch."

When he was satisfied, she buckled the cinch and stepped back.

"Place your left foot into the stirrup, bend that other leg a little and hoist yourself up."

Jenna bent her leg, placing her foot into the stirrup. She turned her foot forward, so that the inside of her foot ran alongside the horse.

"Push off that leg and swing into the saddle," Sam urged.

Jenna didn't realize how many muscles and how much coordination it took to get on a horse. Although she was in good shape, her leg felt the strain. She balanced on her right foot and tried to spring on the ball to heft herself up. The operative word was *tried*.

She made it just about as far as Black Spot's ribs.

"I am so glad that I can be a source of amusement for you," she stated when she heard the choking sounds coming from the front of the horse.

Not to be daunted, Jenna tried again to swing into the saddle, but she couldn't get enough leverage. Suddenly, a set of strong, familiar hands gripped her around the waist and lifted her so that she could swing her leg around.

"I could have done it eventually."

"Yeah, but I couldn't handle staring at your exquisitely tight butt in those jeans anymore or mine would be too tight to ride."

Jenna saw frank appraisal in those eyes. Sam didn't even bother to hide the desire he was feeling. It shone in his intense blue eyes and made her squirm in the saddle. "Is Black Spot a boy or a girl?"

The corner of Sam's mouth crooked just a little. "He's a gelding.

The little smile made her insides turn to weak jelly. "What does that mean?" she asked, trying to gather her composure.

Sam looked off into the distance, as if figuring the most civilized way to answer her question. He used his index finger to push his hat back, so he could look up at her. "Technically he's a male, without his working parts."

"Ouch."

"Makes them docile and really good riding horses."

Jenna snorted. "I can see why. He's probably afraid of what you'll do to him next."

Sam chuckled, walked to the left side of Silver Shadow and smoothly mounted the horse.

"Show-off," she said, and he laughed.

He gave her a few quick tips on controlling a horse and then they were off riding. Jenna immediately loved it. The slow walk was exactly right for her first time out. It was freeing in a way she couldn't seem to name.

They rode in silence for a few miles because they simply didn't need to talk. But then she saw Sam's back go rigid and he sat up in his saddle. He kicked his horse into a trot and took off down the field.

Black Spot started to trot, too. Jenna's butt bounced in the saddle. She had to admit it wasn't as pleasant as walking had been. When Jenna caught up, Sam was down on the ground next to a prone longhorn. She looked in pain and he had heavy concern on his face. Without any words, she knew the cow was in trouble.

"What can I do to help?"

"Dismount and bring me the rope around my saddle horn. Sam was already stripping off his blue chambray shirt. Jenna dismounted, although a little awkwardly. She grabbed the rope and ran over to Sam. Sam's arm was already deep into the cow's birth canal. "The calf is breech. Damn, Texas Rose is one of my best breeders."

"Why don't you keep her in the barn?"

"Longhorns aren't kept in the barn. They're free-range cattle and usually don't have a problem giving birth because they have such wide birth canals."

Jenna bit her lip and pushed fine hairs out of her eyes. She rolled up her sleeves against the heat of the day. She bent down to the cow and touched her head. The cow's eyes rolled to her, but closed as Jenna stroked the place between her horns. "Poor thing. Sam will help you."

She patted the cow, gently smoothing her hand over the glossy coat.

Sam looked up with a half smile for her nonsense chatter to the cow and his throat constricted at the tender look on her face. He'd give his left arm if she would look at him like that, just once. But with a greedy possessiveness, he knew he could easily become addicted to that look. His gaze fell on her hands stroking the cow, and he couldn't stop his wayward thoughts on how it had felt to have those delicate hands on his body, stroking him in his most sensitive areas. "In my saddlebag are a cell phone and some clean towels. Could you bring them to me?"

Jenna went to the smooth leather and opened one of the bags. She pulled out the items he requested.

She gave a towel to Sam, who made quick work of cleaning himself up. He took the cell phone from her and dialed. "Tooter, it's Sam. Texas Rose is trying to throw a breeched calf. Call the vet. I'm in the back forty, east of the big red barn. Bring him when he gets here."

"You're very fond of Tooter, aren't you?" Jenna asked when he disconnected.

He glanced at her and down at the cow. "Yeah," he agreed reluctantly as if he was too embarrassed to admit it.

"You take good care of him." It wasn't a question.

"He's an old man," Sam said defensively. "He should be taken care of. The work isn't too hard here and he will never go hungry or lack a roof over his head as long as I'm alive." The last sentence was said with firm conviction and Jenna smiled at him.

"I'm not accusing you of beating him, Sam."

Sam remained stubbornly silent, giving his full attention to the cow. Jenna noticed his grim look of determination. She shivered at his icy stare, but couldn't help eyeing his bronzed, taut skin, broad shoulders—smooth and muscular—and all of it flexing and rippling every time he moved. Black hair sprinkled his chest, running down his torso to disappear into the tight jeans hiding the rest of his anatomy.

"Was it Tooter or your father who taught you about cows and horses?" She tried again.

"My father was busy with the running of the ranch. Tooter was more patient in teaching me the more intricate ways of ranching. I learned everything I know about critters from him." Again, that reluctant tone, as if Jenna were interrogating him instead of making conversation.

She also heard the admiration and the bitterness in his voice. What was it about the memory of his father that caused these mixed emotions? She had to know.

She picked up a clean towel and mopped his brow. He smelled good—honest, clean sweat blending with a tangy soap scent. She leaned closer to him, one of her breasts connecting with his side. Her nipples immediately hardened and a burning need unfurled deep inside her like a flower unfurls to the warming rays of the sun.

The clear sky gave them no relief from the sun. Having seen it earlier, Jenna retrieved sunscreen from Sam's saddlebag.

Her clothes seemed suddenly stifling, the air too thick to breathe. Sam's skin was warm and covered with a thin film of sweat. While he was preoccupied with the cow, Jenna began to slather the lotion on his back.

He stilled and shot her a glance over his shoulder. "If you're trying to seduce me, I'm a little busy right now."

It took her a moment to realize that he was joking and it brought a smile to her face. "No. Just trying to look after you."

"I've got to help this calf. It's breech, so we'll have to pull it out once I get hold of its hind feet," he said.

She wiped her hands on one of the towels and put the lotion aside.

"Jenna, take this rope and hold it for a minute." Sam felt around and Texas Rose lowed softly in pain, jerking against Sam's intrusion. Jenna soothed her.

"Got him. Give me the rope." He attached the rope and tied it. "Okay, help me, Jenna. Pull as hard as you can, but steady. Don't jerk."

She grasped the rope and helped Sam pull the newborn calf out of his mother's womb. She looked down at the wet, still calf and asked with wonderment, "Is he all right?"

Sam used one of the towels to wipe the animal down. "He's fine." He looked over at Texas Rose and frowned. "She should have stopped writhing and gotten to her feet to nurse and clean the calf."

"Sam, what's wrong?" she asked when she saw the concerned look on his face.

"She should be up now, unless—oh shoot!" He went back down to the cow's abdomen and felt around. "Twins. She's having another one."

Jenna was delighted as she divided her attention between the floundering calf and the cow's lower body.

"This one's not breeched. He's coming out just fine." Texas Rose gave one tightened jerk and the second, smaller calf slipped out. Unlike his brother, this one didn't move.

"Damn." Sam leaned down and touched the little calf, his face turning bleak.

Jenna bit her lip, feeling tears gather at the back of her throat as she watched Sam's face turn to despair.

"Oh, Sam, no," she whispered. And like the fighter she likened him to, he refused to let the little calf die. He opened her mouth, cleaned out the mucus and pushed on her chest, rubbing her vigorously. Compelled, Jenna began to help.

Time ticked by and, with each second, Jenna felt her heart sink. Just when she was about to admit defeat, the little animal sucked in a huffing breath.

The mother rose and began cleaning the newborn calves. Sam checked the second calf. "Yehaw. She gave me a couple of fine bulls." When she had finished cleaning the two small animals, he led first one, then the other to her to nurse.

They were quiet as Sam shrugged back into his shirt and helped Jenna mount. When they got back to the barn, Sam called the vet and told him that tomorrow would be fine to check out the cow and calves. Jenna could hear the pride in his voice. Wondering if she could see the animals from the loft, she climbed the ladder and unlatched the door, pushing it open. A soft breeze wafted in and Jenna craned her neck, trying to spot the new mother and her offspring.

Her boot slipped and, with a cry, she grasped the side of the door. Steel hands grabbed her around the waist and hauled her back against a hard, hot chest.

"What in tarnation do you think you're doing?"

She turned to find herself in Sam's tight embrace. He had a dangerous gunslinger look she'd never seen before. As if he would fight anything to keep her safe. "Is that a Texas Ranger thing?"

He frowned, not happy with her answer. "What?"

"Keeping me from getting hurt?"

"Shoot, woman. You are the most exasperating female I've ever met. I was trying to keep you from plunging headfirst down onto the hard ground, but maybe I shouldn't have worried about it, because your hard head would have saved you."

She pulled away from him to look him in the face, highly amused. "Women are supposed to be mysterious and baffling. It adds to our mystique and keeps men on their toes.''

''Is that what you're doing, keeping me on my toes?'' He cupped her face and slid his thumb along the creamy skin of her cheek. ''Well, you're doing a bang-up job of it. That's for sure,'' he said quietly.

He touched her lightly, caressing her skin, and the look in his eyes sent her heart fluttering.

''I want you, Sam.''

She smiled as she watched him get all churned up. There was something going on with him, something that she liked. He cared about her, whether he wanted to admit it or not. She could see it in his eyes. He wanted her. It thrilled her down to her toes, and at the same time terrified her. She thought about the diary and the way the courtesan had described pleasuring a man.

She moved closer to him, her hand dropping down to the juncture of his jeans. She cupped him through the tight denim.

Her breath caught and moved shallowly in her lungs. She shut her eyes and unintentionally touched her tongue to her lips. Something liquid pooled through her belly to her lower body and settled heavily and with unmistakable hunger in the cleft below her mound.

She heard him release his breath, as if a fist had slammed into his chest. She opened her eyes and watched him watch her. In the dim loft, his eyes were alive and dark with danger. He rubbed his hands roughly over his face. He breathed deeply, his chest rising and falling quickly. He swallowed and his fists curled so tightly that his knuckles pushed against his skin.

"Jenna." He whispered her name, the air in the barn thick with their need.

Without removing her hand, she said softly, "Take off your shirt." Sam's hands unclenched and he started on the first buttons, baring his sun-warmed skin to her. Before he discarded the garment, she leaned forward and touched her mouth to his collarbone. She inhaled sharply, her mouth burning. She bared her teeth and bit him gently. He groaned softly, leaning into her.

His erection was firm and pulsing beneath her hand. With her free hand she unzipped his jeans and pushed them off his hips.

A sweet ache settled in Jenna's heart as she pressed against his taut skin. God, how she wanted him, but not just for the short term. She wanted him forever and ever.

Impossible.

She watched his face as her body flowed down his, her hands cupping his erection.

Sam stilled and Jenna wanted to take his hard lips. The look on his face was violent, and a muscle in his jaw flexed. He grabbed her by her shirtfront, drew her up, and close. So close she could feel his breath on her lips. She couldn't help the shiver of need that coursed through her.

She fought him, wanting to take him into her mouth.

He leaned down and bit her lip with a gentle tug and Jenna thought she would swoon. With his tongue, he laved her flesh between his teeth and she groaned. He let go, replacing the tingling sensation with a wrenching heat as his tongue ran along her mouth. He said, "Do you want to have your way with me?"

"Yes," she said breathlessly, and ducked under his arm. But Sam had other ideas. He grabbed her around her waist and swung her over his shoulder while Jenna kicked and struggled. "No. Here in the hay. Please, Sam," Jenna demanded, and Sam set her on her feet, then trapped her back against his granite chest, his strong, lean hips, and his muscled-to-perfection thighs.

Heat. Everywhere he touched her body brought scorching heat, burning within and without. Sam shuddered with it, his body pressing deeper into hers. Jenna writhed with it and turned away from Sam. Afraid of that heat, she wanted to escape, yet oddly yearned to be consumed by it.

The feel of Sam pressed solidly against her back, her derriere, and the backs of her thighs made her want to scream with her need for him. His breath was hot on the back of her neck, inches away from her skin, sensitized almost to the point of insanity. His touch branded her. Beautiful, callused fingers trailed over her neck and shoulders, moved with aching slowness down the ridge of her spine. His hands finally spread out to loop around the flare of her hips encased in the tight jeans.

A low sound escaped her as he pressed his hard length against her back, where she could feel his arousal with aching clarity.

"In the hay isn't exactly civilized, Jenna," he

rasped. She twisted against him, the unvoiced cry trapped inside her as he moved his hips slowly. His mouth lowered to sweep the hollow where her neck flowed into her shoulder, his tongue moving in slow, delicious circles over her skin. When his hands left her hips to slide over her belly and capture her breasts, the sound of her pleasure, her passion, came from her throat as a gasping, tearing sound of need.

"But it turns you on," she said provocatively.

Her breasts ached for his touch and she inhaled sharply as his hands roughly pulled the shirt from the waistband of her jeans, slid up her rib cage and, with a quick, deft motion, unsnapped her bra where it met between her breasts. Her nipples were ready and erect when he finally cupped them in his big, rough, hot hands. His mouth descended to her ear, his voice straining as he sucked her lobe, sending prickles of fire to the tips of her breasts. She arched into him with a moaning cry. "Tell me it turns you on, too," he demanded, moving beyond control and dragging Jenna with him, with those spoken words.

She cried out again and arched farther into him, the wall of his chest an unmovable, burning hardness against her back. As he took the nipples between his fingers, pinching and tugging on them, Jenna thought it was more than she could take. She struggled and he let her turn so that she was facing him. His eyes blazed with a hard, unyielding fire that reached out and burned her. She gasped at the magnificence of him, his dark, unruly hair. She reached up and ran her fingers through it and he closed his eyes as if in agony.

Without opening them, his mouth descended and captured hers, his lips demanding her to surrender, to submit to him, to give him all that she had to give. But Jenna would surrender later. Right now, she wanted something from him and she was going to get it.

Her hand slid down the taut muscle of his torso to his groin. He moaned hard into her mouth, his hips jerking as her hand curled around his cock.

''Jenna. Oh, God…Jen.'' His voice sounded hoarse in the still air of the barn.

She moved her hand up and felt his body bolt in the way he uncontrollably thrust his hips toward her. His knees buckled and he caught himself against one wall, his palms flat for balance. His chest heaved in and out and she stroked his jaw with the lightest of touches. She didn't want to break his pleasure by distracting him. He was putty in her hands and she took full advantage of it. She pressed against him. Looking up into his face, contorted with feeling, only intensified her desire for the smoothness, the heat of him in her mouth.

When her lips encompassed the head of his penis, he whispered a curse, his hips bucking, his legs quaked and he leaned harder into the wall so that his chest muscles stood out in stark relief. Her hum of pleasure against the hot skin her lips caressed brought a tight groan from him. Bowing at the waist, his restless leg rubbed against her arm, the silkiness of his inner thigh encouraging.

She grasped the base of his shaft and swirled her tongue around the head, laving him until he swore low and vehemently under his breath. Grabbing her by the shoulders, he pulled her up his body. For a split second, he looked into her eyes and she shivered at the dangerous passion there.

He took the ends of her shirt and jerked it up her body, baring her breasts to him, lifting her easily, his biceps bulging from the weight of her. She brought her hands up to clasp his wrists, sliding seductively over the smooth hair on his forearms until she reached the tight, rounded muscles. She tested his taut skin and felt the strength of him pulsate into her fingers until the maleness of him seemed to seep into her blood and burn.

For a moment of heated silence he just stared at her. Then he caught a nipple between his teeth. He licked and sucked until she arched in desperate, aching need, causing little frissons of heat to explode in her stomach. It was a sensation that reached into the core of her, stabbing so intensely she was afraid she was beginning to unravel.

Finally, giving in to her need to touch him, she ran her hands through that endearing head of hair, liking the soft feel of the strands against her fingers. Enjoying it so much she did it again, much more slowly. Her knees went weak. Desire rushed through her body, hot and thick.

''Damn,'' he whispered raggedly before his mouth was on hers, urgently pressing her backward, grabbing her around the waist, bowing her over his arm. Soon, his hands were deftly at her jeans and underwear, and she stepped out of them.

At last, she knew what it was like to be really

kissed by him. This was why he kept such a firm control over himself. He had found a well of passion that he hadn't realized existed. It reached out and engulfed him as easily as a tidal wave engulfed an island with an unrelenting force. The same force that crashed over her.

The heat of his mouth seared every other kiss she'd ever had permanently from her memory. As kisses went, this one was off the scale. There was no point in grading, where Sam was concerned.

He deepened the kiss, his sensuous lips flexing over hers in an urgent fierceness that left her breathless. She felt him spread his heavily muscled thighs to give him better balance. He slid his big hands over her buttocks, jerking her hips against him.

The pulsing heat from his groin reached out to her, made her groan into his soft lips.

The groan tightened his body, and even as he cursed himself for his lack of control, something inside cried out with aching clarity—she was so exquisitely right for him, it was criminal. She fit to him like a perfectly fashioned suit, like a glove fit a hand, like a woman was supposed to fit a man.

He had no idea what he wanted from her except to bury himself in her so deeply he would be lost. He didn't know why he was so attracted to her, why only she could ignite these primal urges.

The more he kissed her, the more he wanted. The need careened around inside him until he growled deep in his throat and pushed her down into the pile of hay.

He'd refused to dull the ache with alcohol, resisting

the urge to drink himself into a stupor over a woman. The truth of the matter was he'd been afraid to pick up a bottle, afraid that a penchant for alcohol would consume him. He couldn't hide. He had to deal with his emotions and his needs. Yet, in those agonizing days he'd had some insight into his father's torture, a thread of understanding how seductive it could be to use alcohol to deaden white-hot, all-encompassing desire.

He slid his hips against her slim ones, while he softened the kiss, to woo rather than to conquer.

It was Sam's undoing when her mouth moved over his in such obvious worship, like a woman paying homage to something beyond her comprehension, something so enchanting and captivating that it defied human understanding. He felt the strength of her arousal and moved against her with an abandon that startled him.

When Sam kissed her, he sensed an innocence, as if she hadn't been kissed like this before, had never felt this twisting passion that was eating him up. As if she were untried. It couldn't be possible, as he felt her melt into him and her reaction shattered every other thought apart like glass splintering into tiny crystal shards.

She sighed against his mouth as the wet heat of his tongue came up against her parted lips, which she opened eagerly. She moaned as his tongue explored her mouth possessively, expertly, running it around the silky sweetness, moaning more when her tongue entwined with his, stroking, tasting, begging for more, much more. Her scent was intoxicating, very feminine, very seductive.

"Now, Sam." He planted his palms on either side of her, and plunged into her with deep, uncontrollable thrusts. He had no finesse left, no self-control. It was raw, base and wild. She started to come before he bottomed out. He felt her contracting around him, heard her breathy gasps spiraling several octaves higher, and pure satisfaction exploded through him. Holding himself deep even as the need to climax beat at him, he ground against her as he felt her climax go on and on and on. All he knew for certain was the feel of her coming apart beneath him was the biggest turn-on he'd ever felt.

When her orgasm tapered off, he began to pump steadily in smooth, hard strokes. Jenna wrapped her legs around his hips and moved in concert with him, and he sucked in a breath.

He thrust two, three, four times and came in a blinding, clenching, white-hot pulsation after pulsation.

Moments later, shuddering with satisfaction, he eased down on top of her. He held her to him and rolled to his side, filled with a ferocious possessiveness.

It made him uneasy, for possessiveness wasn't an emotion he'd expected to feel. Since Tiffany had left him and he'd sworn that he would never get involved with a woman like her again, he was filled with the need to run. Now he was filled with the need to pull Jenna close and never let her go. But it was never up to him. He'd learned that and accepted it. Tiffany had eventually stayed away until they didn't have a marriage at all. Here he was again, in that same wagon, knowing he had nothing to offer Jenna that could compete with her rich lifestyle.

He was simply a rancher and an uncomplicated guy. Yet he felt entangled and a surprising sense of completeness.

Even though it was tinged with dread.

10

THE CRASH OF THUNDER woke her and she jumped against Sam's side. She sat upright, realizing that while they had slept in the sunny meadow after their lunch break, a nasty storm had rolled over them.

A day had passed since the twin calves had been born, and Sam had worked diligently with Tooter so that Sam had the time to show her around his ranch.

Sam sat up next to her, looking at the sky. "I listened to the weather report earlier and it was supposed to be clear all day. But that's what happens near the gulf. Storms can come in suddenly and catch you off guard. Let's put the stuff together. I'll get the horses."

Sam left her and Jenna quickly collected the leftover meal and returned it to the saddlebag. Fighting against the hard wind, she picked up the blanket. It flapped and wound around her like something alive. A crack of lightning pierced the leaden sky and Jenna heard the frightened whinny of a horse. She wrestled the blanket away from her body in time to see Shadow rear. With horror, she realized that Sam was too close to the horse.

But he didn't hesitate, nor did he run from the animal. Jenna's heart was in her throat as Sam tried to calm the skitterish stallion. A peal of thunder and another crack of lightning hit close to the tree the horses were tied to. It was too much for the already frightened animal. He reared again, pulling at the tied reins and they snapped free. The front hooves, dangerously close to Sam's head, flicked out and caught him across the temple. He grabbed his head and reeled back as the stallion shot out of the meadow and into the deepening gloom.

Jenna dropped the blanket and it went swirling away into the storm. When she reached Sam, he was swearing a blue streak.

"That stallion never did like storms."

"Sam, your head! Are you okay?" She touched the bloody spot but could barely see where the steel-shod hoof had made contact with his head.

"I'm fine. Just clipped me. Get the saddlebags," he hollered over the rushing wind. Jenna ran back to the leather bags and over to Sam. The Appaloosa danced at the ends of the reins, his eyes rolling. With a quick flick of his wrist, Sam pulled the reins free and, with one lithe movement, mounted the horse. He took the bags from her and settled them on Spot's hindquarters.

He reached down his hand and Jenna looked up at him. The blood slid slowly down his face, his blue eyes stood out like a beacon in the raging storm. Her heart shifted in her chest and slowly beat, once, twice, three times. She reached up and grasped his hand.

"Bend your knees and jump," he yelled over the storm. Jenna did as he said and, with brute strength, Sam pulled her up behind him. She clutched at the horse, even though there wasn't any way she could have slid off, cushioned as she was by Sam's body. Raindrops stung her cheeks. The cold wind beat against her. But she had to close her eyes against the surprising warmth in her belly, the tight pleasure in her chest at the feeling of Sam against her.

"We should have taken the damn truck."

"What fun would that have been? Touring your ranch in a four-wheel-drive. How boring."

He laughed. "You surprise me every minute, Jenna. We'll have to find shelter. It's too far to get to the ranch."

"Where?"

"There's a line shack not far from here." At his words, the world went gray and a deluge hit them with the force of a battering ram. Jenna was immediately soaked through to the skin and could barely catch her breath at the cold rain.

For about a minute, she fought the urge to sink against him, and then she gave up the fight. He held her arm around him with a quiet competence, not too tight, not too loose. Jenna felt safe, the rocking motion of the horse soothing. The world around them was swirling, but Sam protected her like precious cargo.

Jenna lifted her head a little and tried to see through the rain. All she saw was a misty landscape with no distinguishable landmarks, at least not to her. There was just the pelting rain and the heavy, cold wind. Spot moved along at a good pace, his hooves muffled by the wet grass and mud.

Sam pulled her tighter against him, afraid of what would happen if he lost his grip and she fell from the horse. He blamed himself for his stupidity in letting them get caught like this.

He gave Spot his head, knowing the animal could instinctively find shelter, just as Sam knew he was moving in the right direction. It must be his cowboy instinct or his horse sense.

Just then Spot came to a shuddering halt. Sam pulled his eyes from her and focused his attention ahead of them. "Hey, boy," he crooned, his voice hesitant, his attention on the storm in front of them, his hand stroking the horse. Was it danger Spot had sensed?

Spot quivered. His head was up, his ears flicking forward. Suddenly, the big horse let out a long, shrill whinny and broke into a trot. If Sam hadn't been holding on, Jenna would have met the ground.

And Sam suddenly knew it wasn't danger. Through the rushing downpour, the horse had gotten a whiff of hay and oats. "Atta boy," Sam praised the animal, leaning into the gait. That was all the encouragement Spot needed to leap almost to a full-out gallop.

"Are we here?" Jenna yelled.

"We're close," Sam said, directly into her ear. Then it was all he could do to concentrate on his riding as the line shack started to take shape in the pouring rain.

When they hit the barn, the hail pelted them as Sam quickly dismounted and pulled at the small barn doors. His slick fingers slipped on the metal lock as he pulled keys out of his back pocket. Finally, the lock sprung and he pulled open the doors. He grabbed the reins and led the horse inside. Jenna ducked as they cleared the doorway. Sam went to her and grabbed her by the waist, he helped her to dismount.

He handed her his key ring. "Go up to the shack and unlock the door. I'll bed Spot down and get the generator going. There are dry clothes in the bedroom closet. Get changed."

Jenna took the keys and put them into her pocket. She pulled the saddlebags off the horse and threw them over her shoulder.

She brushed past him and went to Spot. She gently rubbed at his forehead, and if the big gelding had been a cat he would have begun to purr. She whispered, "Thanks for getting us here."

Then she moved toward Sam and stopped in front of him. "Thank you, too." She tried to smile, but her mouth only turned up at the corners.

"Come here," he said gruffly.

He opened his arms and she walked to him. He drew her up in a firm embrace, burying her face against the curve of his neck. Sam felt her inhale raggedly as she burrowed deeper into the hollow between his neck and shoulder. With a shaky sigh, she slid her arms around his waist. Pressing a gentle kiss to her temple, he slid his fingers along her wet scalp, dislodging her hat. Cradling her head in his firm grip, the heavy, wet silk of her hair tangled around his fingers. Sam closed his eyes and hugged her hard, a wave of reaction making his chest constrict. Shoot, but she filled up something that was empty and aching inside him.

He felt her take another deep, relaxing breath, and he smoothed one hand up her back, holding her tightly against him. Easing in a tight breath of his own, he brushed a kiss against her temple, then spoke, his voice husky and rough. "You're welcome."

A shiver flowed through her and Jenna slipped her arms around his neck, the alteration in her stance bringing her flush against him. Sam drew an unsteady breath and angled her head back, making a low, indistinct sound as he covered her mouth in a kiss that was raw, dictated by the need to soothe and encourage. Jenna went still. Then, with a muffled gasp, she clasped him and gave in to his profound, reassuring kiss. She moved against him, and Sam shuddered and tightened his hold, a rage of delight moving through him like the strong beat of his heart. Making him wish, ah shoot, wishing he could draw her right inside him and keep her there forever.

Pulling his mouth away, he looked down into her eyes. "Now, get yourself into that shack and put some dry clothes on, greenhorn."

She smiled this time and reached out and caressed his face. Ducking down to grab her hat, she left the barn, running out into the storm.

For a moment he couldn't move. The caress along his jaw wasn't sexual in any way, but it had shaken him like a tremor. Shook him more than a blatant sexual move would ever have. It was an emotional connection and, for some reason, Sam felt as if he'd just been let out of a dark, tight space, as if he could finally take his first breath.

He had received something from her that he hadn't expected. An extraordinary gift and it unsettled him.

IT TOOK SAM twenty minutes to strip the saddle and bridle from the horse, give him water, feed and hay from the supplies kept at all the line shacks on his property. Then he went into the storm to where he kept the generator and started its motor. By then, hail the size of golf balls was hitting the tin roof constantly.

Although he referred to these havens in the wilds of the back forty as shacks, they were more like old-fashioned log cabins made quite comfortable to pass the time in if there happened to be a sudden blizzard, or, in this case, a tropical storm.

He opened the cabin door and was greeted with a blazing fire. A pan of beans was already heating and Jenna was wringing out her hair in the sink in the kitchen. He stood for a moment in the doorway, another one of his stereotypes going down the tubes. It didn't look as if she'd had any problem starting the fire and figuring out what their priorities were. He could see how she shivered, and another realization hit him with the force of a horse's kick right in the gut. She'd forgone her own comfort to set the blaze and get something hot for them to eat. Tiffany would have already been in dry clothes, complaining about the cold, waiting for him to set the fire and cook the food.

The thought made him gruff. "I told you to get out of those clothes."

Jenna stiffened at his tone. "I assumed it was more important to start a fire and get some food going." She wanted friction between them and leaped at the chance to spar with him. The embrace, the kiss, the sheer tenderness of that moment in the barn had rocked her, terrified her, made her crave for distance between them.

She was here to get that damn diary that was now like a weight around her neck. She found it harder and harder to remember the real reason she was visiting Texas. Every time Sam got within a few feet of her, she couldn't seem to remember her own name. He was multifaceted, gorgeous, interesting as hell and she wanted, craved, to know more about him. And that shamed her because she'd promised her gran that she would get that diary. Instead, she'd slept with Sam and enjoyed his company for days. She could assuage her guilt a little since she'd made two tries to get to the desk and Sam had thwarted both attempts.

She turned to the sink and reached for the tap, but Sam was there. "Don't touch that. Stay away from the all water faucets, and sinks. Metal pipes can transmit electricity and there's still plenty of activity out there."

"I need water for coffee."

"You need to get out of those clothes."

Jenna put her hands on her hips. "Okay, I will, but I'll need some hot, strong coffee after I've changed."

He sighed and she had to fight the urge to touch him. He went to a cupboard and opened it. Inside were numerous full-to-the-gallon plastic containers of water.

"You really believe in being prepared. I found batteries, a radio, candles, a flashlight with batteries, canned goods and firewood, all easy to access."

"And you had no problem setting the fire."

"No, I have a fireplace in New York." She grabbed up one of the water jugs and proceeded to make coffee in his old electric percolator. "I also found a first-aid kit. We should take care of your forehead."

After opening a drawer and pulling out that first-aid kit and a soft cloth, she placed the kit on the countertop. "Grab one of those jugs." He hefted a jug and walked back to the counter.

"Clothes first, doctoring second."

He turned and, before she could protest, grabbed her arm and pulled her into the tiny bedroom. He left her standing in the center of the room as he rummaged through drawers. "Get your clothes off, Jenna."

Jenna tried. She began to fumble with the buttons on her shirt. Her fingers felt thick and achy, and she couldn't seem to get a purchase on the buttons. Sam turned with his arms full of clothes.

"Here," he commanded, already out of his coat, his jeans just as wet as hers. For some reason, though, he wasn't shivering. Jenna couldn't understand it. Slinging his cache over his shoulder, Sam reached for her shirt and freed a few buttons. "I'll do it."

Jenna stiffened abruptly, the thought of Sam doing something so intimate wormed right through her.

"No," she protested, forcing her fingers to try to latch on to a button. "No, I'll do it."

But her fingers slid purposelessly across the button.

Sam pushed her hands away and impaled her with his best glare. "Darlin', you are stubborn. Let me do something for you. I got you in this predicament in the first place."

Jenna closed her eyes, too shaken by Sam's proximity to face him. He stripped off her shirt and then unsnapped and unzipped her jeans. Jenna could feel the quick brush of those fingers against her breasts. She wished he would touch her in a more sexual way, because this concern for her was almost too much to bear, especially since she was here under false pretenses. She didn't want Sam to care for her. She wanted him to be one of those males that gave her sex and sent her on her merry way. Why did he have to be so sweet?

"I don't know if these pants will fit around your hips."

That opened her eyes. "Are you calling me fat?"

He grinned a real grin. The kind two people trade who've shared something special or perilous. "Well, shoot no. I was just thinking that most of these things are for guys and, well—" his gaze went down her body "—you ain't, well, a guy."

Jenna dropped onto the edge of the bed, warmed more by his smile than by any fireplace or dry cotton. Feeding on that smile, she savored it like first sunlight.

He went down on his knee in front of her, pulled off her boots, the wet jeans and underwear. He sorted through the pile of clothes and found a pair of sweatpants. "I think these will fit around your hips." He gave her a snide grin.

"Don't start on my hips again, Sam."

He handed her a cotton undershirt and a sweatshirt. He stood and stripped and put on dry clothes.

Then it was to the kitchen and the hot coffee flavored with cloves. It warmed her down to her toes.

Soon she found herself sitting on the couch in front of the fire with the water, cloth and first-aid kit.

Before he could protest, she took his chin and angled his cut temple for her scrutiny. It wasn't deep, but it was angry and red. The rain had washed off most of the blood so that the cut oozed slowly. She gently bathed the blood away.

The warmth of his face made her knees weak and her hand reached out to grope for the first-aid kit. At this moment she desperately needed something to hang on to.

Her mind went back to a calendar that one of her friends at Julliard had hanging in her little one-room apartment. She had been from Wyoming and Jenna guessed the calendar was a reminder of home. Each month depicted a cowboy stud and June had featured a particularly rugged one. The caption had read I'm The Kind of Man Your Mother Warned You About.

And how. Her mother didn't need to tell her this man was too wild, raw, untamed. She could feel the danger in him—feel the lethal quality hum through her body, pump through her veins potent and heady.

You shouldn't be daydreaming, a little voice said caustically in her head. Looking into his eyes, she knew suddenly she'd have plenty to daydream about now. She felt as if she could drown in his dark blue eyes. Warm, expressive eyes. Yet she knew the moment she got the diary in her hands, she'd be gone.

She was a grown woman, not some child who didn't know the score. An overwhelming sense of protectiveness flooded over her. No, she wasn't a child.

She put the cloth down on the coffee table and pulled apart the wrapping for a butterfly bandage. She pressed the bandage to his temple. Her hand remained on his face though, feathering lightly over his skin. His rough, callused hand came up and covered hers. The gaze he leveled at her was hypnotic, steady and seductive, his eyes burning liquid blue.

"Aren't you going to kiss it and make it all better?" he asked, tilting his head in an adorable way.

The weakness in her knees seemed to radiate throughout her whole body with slow languid fingers encompassing all her traitorous muscles.

She moved forward, close to his face, and kissed his bandaged head. "All better?"

She stared at him. She couldn't help it. He was much too fascinating for her own good. Her mind went back to that calendar. That picture of the handsome cowboy had also included a wolf in the background. She was reminded of that graceful gray wolf sighting prey in those fierce, hungry eyes.

She now found out what it was to be the prey.

Sam's touch felt like no other man's as he trailed his fingertips down her arm. Her breath trembled at the electric sensation of his bare flesh against hers. The rain pounded against the roof in a comforting beat.

Like the hard beat of her heart against her breastbone, it was so loud she was sure Sam could hear it.

The fire roared as small sparks exploded into the

air and were consumed by the blaze. The wind picked up and rattled against the walls of the shack, water dripped in a slow cadence in the sink. Around them the air seethed with a tangible force. Something alive. It smelled of hearth and home. It sounded like the cry of rapture. It felt like the hot, taut skin of a lover.

Very gently, Sam placed kisses over her face, rubbed at her bottom lip with the rough pad of his thumb. He was so close to her that she could see the thick, lush length of his eyelashes as they fluttered closed, hiding his intense gaze from her. His hard jaw beckoned her hand, masculine, with a dark stubble that made him appear just a notch sexier. As if he needed that.

Jenna reached up and drew her hand through his hair, and his chest lifted in a little sigh. Something deep inside her thawed. Something so long frozen, Jenna never even knew it existed. Sam's eyelids fluttered open and Jenna lost herself in the depth of his vibrant gaze.

His strong arms came around her in a tight embrace, the fresh rain-washed smell of him wrapped around her senses, traveled deep inside her and twirled around her heart. His mouth traveled in a slow, seductive slide. He kissed her lobe, whispered her name, the sound of it like a prayer.

In the depths of his eyes his desire shimmered in stark open view, a shimmer that was mirrored and built in her own soul. There was also wariness, protection and distance that she was aware he found difficult to maintain.

"Jenna…"

His voice rasped, overcome with his need. Jenna shivered with the answering plea on her lips. She watched the loneliness in his eyes shift like ghostly shadows. She heard the irregular tempo of his breathing, felt the fine edge of his vulnerability and sensed the unraveling of his control, as hers simply broke free from her.

Her heart knew him, and it was inevitable that they would come to this moment in time. She'd peeled away his defenses and crept close for a peek inside him, knowing that whatever it was that made up Sam Winchester played at her like the ancient music of passion, bonding, intimacy. She'd demanded from him without words, intuitively drawing him to what could perhaps be his downfall as well as her own.

It might not be prudent or smart, but it was what she craved. And she'd known it deep inside for a long time.

There was incredible character in this man, born of the code of the West, ingrained and unapologetic. But there was hot, turbulent need, a need so great it could overwhelm her.

That need, freed from its bonds, flashed over her, igniting her own desire with the tinder of his mouth, the kindling of his hands, the scorching heat of his body. His mouth moved over hers in a dazzling, sighing blending that left them enveloped in each other's arms. It whipped up flames that seared her, that propelled her to answer Sam's intensity with her own.

He crushed her to him. He lifted a hand and cupped her face, tilted her head back so that he could slake his thirst with her. His fingers were rough, but the whisper of his breath on her was as sweet as honey. The thunder of his heart shuddered through her. The solid wall of his chest comforted her and tormented her. Jenna lifted her own hands, sought the hard ridge of muscle, the devastating heat of skin, the overwhelming feel of surrender. Her insides staggered with the capacity of his heart, vibrated with the power of him, dissolved with the compassion of him.

His hands were impatient, his mouth greedy, his body eager. Jenna absorbed it all and it went to her head like potent wine. She reeled with the intoxication of it. His comforting arms, his broad shoulders, his taut chest. So solid, so sleek, brushed with firelight and shadow, so supple beneath her seeking hands. His hips slid hard and aching against hers.

He bent a little, one arm sweeping down her back as he gathered her up in his arms.

"In front of the fire, Sam."

He turned to look at the blaze and when his eyes returned to hers, they were smoldering. He took pillows from the couch, his muscles delineated in the glow from the fire. He spread them on the floor, along with the soft blanket that had been thrown across the back of the couch.

Sam wrapped her in his arms and buried his face in her damp hair as they stumbled together to the makeshift bed in front of the fire.

In Jenna's secret heart, in the worst days of the sheer loneliness, she had wished for warmth and light. Her imagination could never have predicted the reckless feel of Sam's hunger. She'd only hoped for the seductive heat, the sizzling union of a man and a woman.

She discovered that night what it cost her to give what she had never given before. She sank to the floor, tangled in Sam, her body knotted with wonder, marveling at the connection her heart made with Sam's.

With hands made unsteady by need, he stripped himself, then her. He took her nipples, his mouth insistent, arousing and almost unbearable. He suckled, caressed, nipped, until Jenna scored his back with her eagerness. She bucked against him, writhed beneath him, delighting in the rasp of hair against the sleek skin of her belly. Devastated by the pulse of him against her.

His mouth was a hot brand against her skin, always present against her breasts, her throat and her belly. He paid special attention to her mouth. His kisses lashed her, showing her no mercy, making her surge to heart-pounding life. She tasted cloves and coffee on his tongue and smelled the rain in his hair.

No man had ever brought her to such life, had ever driven her to such torment. No man had ever whispered her name as if his life depended on it.

Jenna melded with Sam. She was drowning in him, soaring with him. The frenzy he roused in her belly lashed her, flayed her, whipped her, until sensation sang through her blood, sparkled in her fingertips and toes, danced in her eyes.

She felt his shaft, hard and insistent against her thigh, and she opened for him, spreading her legs wide to take him against the wet, scorching heat of her core. She heard his moan when the smooth head of his shaft first touched her, jolting her with fevered anticipation.

He slid down her body, dragging his mouth over her aching flesh; she arched into his kisses, writhing in the throes of hard-pounding pleasure.

She groaned, groaned again. The peak was building in her, clambering against her belly, jagged and thudding in her. His mouth took her soaring, spinning, balancing her on a knife's edge. On the verge of fulfillment, she wept with it. Her head lashed from side to side, her body convulsing, shuddering as the pleasure sped through her in exquisite sensation after sensation.

She opened her eyes. She saw the inferno of satisfaction, the need in Sam's eyes, the frayed limit of control, the gloss of sweat on his forehead and the stunning smile that was hers. And then she reached to him, taking him in her hand. His face contorted in agony, his hard, chest-deep moan echoing against the walls of the cabin. She saw his eyes widen, darken. She smiled then, and guided him to her.

She cried out, the agony of his penetration incredible, the thrusts of his hips excruciating. She clutched at him, dragged her own hands through his hair and demanded her own kisses. She pulled him against her, hard and urgent, and blatantly urged him on.

Sam grasped her hips, increasing the tempo, powering into her, slick and hot and sweet. His thrusts plumbed fathomless depths, more infinite than passion, want, isolation or desire could reach. All Jenna could do was take him deeper. She bowed and swayed, her hands holding him tight, his hands and his mouth devouring her. She felt his cock grow harder inside her. And then, suddenly, like a white-hot storm, the fire whooshed over her in breathtaking waves of flame. Her equilibrium broke into shards, splinters, dust. She cried out to him, caught in a vortex of feeling, sensation, detonation. He cried out and followed her into that storm, a harsh sound of pleasure. She held him tighter, tighter, whispering to him as he buried himself in her, as he, too, shuddered to release.

She gasped against the pulsing aftermath of the passion, and they lay tangled and spent. His forehead connected with hers, his chest heaving from his exertion. She fondled his damp hair, taking pleasure in the heaviness of him, the heat of him, the leashed power of him. She fought the need to pull away; afraid that, once separated, they wouldn't be able to find their way back.

Sam finally rolled to his side. He cushioned her against him, rubbing his cheek against her hair.

"I think we should make our way to the bed, unless you want to sleep here."

"I want to sleep here."

"I'll get more blankets then."

After that coupling, Jenna couldn't imagine ever feeling cold again. But the night would be cold, even with the fire. She wished there was some kind of cover that might protect them from the world, from the dawning of the day and the reality she was going to have to face.

"A good idea," she agreed.

Sam came back with a couple of blankets, pillows and a featherlight down comforter and they snuggled beneath the warmth, wrapped in each other's arms. They were quiet with contentment and pleased with understanding, ignoring the world beyond the fire and the rain and what would await them when they woke.

That would be later, Jenna knew, her eyes closed against Sam's chest, her fingers entwined in his, her leg thrown over his. For now, she couldn't ask more than to savor these few moments of perfect and intense passion.

11

SAM WATCHED JENNA from the back of the classroom as she conducted her master class. The students asked numerous questions and Jenna handled each one with poise and confidence. She taught them what she called bowing techniques, using musical terminology he didn't understand.

They had spent the night in the line shack and returned to the ranch at first light. The way she had met the storm and the night roughing it impressed him. She'd also taken to riding as if she'd been born in the saddle, even insisting on managing the grooming of the big Appaloosa herself. He smiled to himself. He had to admit she'd done a damn fine job.

She'd also done a damn fine job of insinuating herself into his heart. He couldn't deny it. She was there and it would take time to get her out. She'd slipped under his defenses and made herself at home. She'd even groomed Silver Shadow when he'd returned after the storm. Now he couldn't imagine sleeping without her, seeing her as he walked through the door, having her smile at him from across the table. But she'd made it quite clear that what she wanted from him was a temporary fling. Nothing more.

It's what he'd wanted, too, but now he wanted

more. Somehow he would have to accept the fact that she didn't. It was Wednesday, and by Saturday she would be gone. She'd committed to two concerts and the final performance would be on Friday.

He got up from his seat and slipped out of the room. He'd do a few errands and then come back and pick her up.

He was better off, he told himself silently. She might do all the things that Tiffany couldn't or wouldn't, but he was aware that she still didn't belong here. He'd be fooling himself if he tried to make himself believe that she did.

JENNA SAID GOODBYE to the last student and exited the classroom, but Sam was nowhere to be found. She went to the entrance and peeked out, but his truck wasn't at the curb. He must be delayed. Jenna went back into the college and sat down on one of the couches in the empty lounge. Opening her briefcase, she noticed the red cover of her grandmother's diary.

She opened to the page she had marked and began to read.

January 30, 1958

Oahu is beautiful and I'm happy to relax after my concerts on the big island of Hawaii. I was invited by the mayor of Oahu to be his guest. His daughter, Kalei, was very kind to me and asked me if I wished to learn the hula. I told her that I thought the dance was very erotic and I'd love to learn.

She gifted me with a colorful swath of material, a grass skirt she had made with her own hands, and a very suggestive, anatomically correct tiki good-luck charm necklace.

One night, after I'd been practicing the hula for about a week, the mayor hosted a luau.

There were many sailors there and Kalei asked if I wished to dance. I offered to sing, too, and learned a beautiful song in Hawaiian that spoke of a forbidden love.

I wore very little, just a simple multicolored strip of material and the grass skirt.

When the drumming began, I could feel the beat deep inside my body to the very core of my sex. I walked onto the stage and began the sinuous, graceful movements. A navy officer sat in the first row and caught my eye. He watched me intently, his eyes following all my movements.

I danced in the traditional way called *Kahiko*. The style is rooted in tradition, in a culture of survival and the laws of the gods and *kapus*, which means taboo. When I began to move, I felt the raw life force that rushed through my body. The steps and movements convey power, sexual prowess, sensuality, and a deep reverence for the balancing forces of nature and the gods, who protect or savage at will. I danced for him, sang the song to him. It was very arousing.

Later, after the festivities, I took a walk on the beach and that navy officer followed me. He told me his name is Daniel. He is very handsome and the adventure changed for me. I can't say how or why, but I knew I couldn't seduce him out here on the beach, even though I wished to.

He is very sweet and kind and said he was on a month's leave. He spoke to me about his loneliness and the draw of the sea. I spent all night listening to him talk about his life.

I'm overcome by emotion. I'm surprised that a man would be interested in only conversation from a woman and not want anything else.

I kissed him softly on the lips, using all that I had learned to not seduce, but to connect. His mouth was full and I couldn't get enough of kissing him.

It was the most amazing night of my tour.

February 28, 1958

I have been so neglectful in writing in my diary, but it's been such a glorious month with Daniel. The first time we made love was magical. It was on a secluded beach with nothing but a blanket beneath our heaving bodies. His mouth, hot on my breasts, felt so glorious.

My hands kneaded the leashed strength bunched in his muscles. The feel of his hard, thick shaft between my legs made me moan into his mouth. I gently took his full bottom lip between my teeth, nipping it tenderly.

I could feel him trembling and he pleaded with me. "Please," he said thickly.

The wild urgency of his kiss vibrated through every pore, every cell, and every muscle with a throbbing, reverberating resonance. I thrust my silk-clad breasts against his bare chest.

His mouth slipped down my neck to my collarbone where he lightly ran his tongue over the velvet ridge. I had twisted against his hold, when I felt the moist teasing of his tongue glide over my skin. His hands settled on my rib cage and I was caught up in a whirlwind of sensation when his hands moved up my rib cage, each delicate wedge of bone by each delicate wedge of bone, until he cupped my breasts, his thumbs caressing the hard tips. His mouth closed over my flesh and I gasped at the sharp, electrifying sensation.

When he entered me I climaxed hard. He thrust into me in an out-of-control passion. Never before have I experienced such a deep, abiding emotion for a man. Never before had I wanted to take a moment in time and freeze it for all eternity.

Afterward I lay in his arms, spent, satisfied and determined to—

"I hope you haven't been waiting long." Sam's deep voice broke her concentration and Jenna jumped, hastily closing the small book.

"I got caught up jawing about longhorn breeding and lost track of the time."

With trembling hands, she replaced the diary and stood. Reaching for Sam by the back of the neck, she brought his mouth down to hers. She tasted his lips slowly and languidly, needing the scent of him in her nostrils, the feel of his big body against hers.

This tough, tantalizing man made her want things that weren't possible. There was no way she would fit in here. No way she could stay here and be true to her music. No way.

And she couldn't bear it if he ended up like her father. To be broken, stamped into the dust under the heel of her mother's unfeeling shoe. Jenna wouldn't destroy Sam. She couldn't give him what he wanted, either—home, hearth and children.

When she broke the kiss, he gave her a long, assessing look. She avoided his gaze and looked at anything but him. She experienced a hefty shot of guilty conscience. She wasn't here for this, the unprecedented emotion she felt for this man. She was here for the diary, and she'd been too long in getting her hands on it. To hell with her gran's search for the perfect passion. The last entry in her gran's diary had been special. She could tell by the depth of emotion in the passage. That encounter had touched Jenna more than she was willing to admit because it seemed that the search wasn't about passion at all. Unlike her gran's encounters, her relationship with Sam wasn't casual. She had tried to make herself believe that, but it wasn't true. This wasn't fun and games, no matter what Jenna thought she was doing.

He held her and made her look at him. "Boy, Jenna, I should be late more often."

Her cheeks heated with a flush. If only she didn't want more from him—more than an easygoing friendship spiced with hot sex. But she did want more. She wanted so much more. Drawing a tremulous breath, she slid her arms around his waist. "Don't get a big head, Winchester."

They walked out of the college into the sunlight. Sam held her door open and she stepped up into the truck.

Sam went through the center of town, and, for the first time, Jenna really looked around. She spotted Lurleen and waved as they passed the Kellar Mercantile and the diner. It was a town rich with history and full of friendship and camaraderie. Just as they were turning a corner, a structure caught her eye. Windy Bill's Honky-Tonk and Saloon was printed on a big neon sign that wasn't lit.

"Sam, what's that? A bar?"

"You could say that. That's the honky-tonk."

"Honky-tonk?"

"A country-western bar and nightclub."

"Do they have dancing there?"

"Sure, the Texas two-step and swing."

"Could you take me?" she asked, intrigued.

"It's not the kind of place you're used to."

His voice was laced with censure and reluctance. He was starting to draw away and she should let him, but it hurt inside. "I'd like to go, unless you're busy tonight."

"I'm not, but if you can wait, Saturday is the best night to go." He took his eyes off the road to look at her.

She met his eyes evenly. "I'll be leaving on Saturday," she said.

"That's right. You are. I forgot," Sam said flatly.

"Are you angry with me?"

She could see an odd play of emotions cross his face in the sunlight. "Why would I be angry?"

"I told you I was staying two weeks. I've got a tour to finish up. I have to be in Rome on Monday. Besides, I've taken up enough of your time."

He held his jaw firmly, his lips compressed, his eyes carefully on the road. "Tooter would agree."

"I bet he would."

"I've got to stop at the feed store and pick up some nutritional supplements. Do you mind?"

"No. Go ahead."

The feed store parking lot was packed with trucks. Some men were loading; others were leaning on the side of their pickups, talking. Sam parked the truck and Jenna opened the door and dropped down to the gravel. Sam was greeted by almost everyone there. He smiled warm and friendly, a smile that crinkled up his eyes and showed the stark white of his teeth against his tanned features. He held out his hand again and again, greeting this neighbor and that with questions about relatives or animals or occupations. And he brought Jenna right along with him, so that she was enfolded into the warmth of the group of men and women.

Jenna could see that each person he greeted was truly glad to see him. The men showed respect, and the women showed the kind of natural maternal pride that tends to hover around a hometown boy who's done well.

And Jenna knew this was where Sam belonged. He was part of the landscape, ingrained in the community, one with the land and the people in a town that he took as his responsibility to nurture.

He was as grounded as she was transient. She had no ties in New York now that her gran was dead, and only an agent friend who cared about her as a person. She'd never really had time to make lasting friendships like this. She'd never find this kind of connection when she returned to her apartment building. In fact, she'd be surprised if anyone even realized she'd been gone.

This kind of connection pulled at her heart and she suddenly longed to belong as solidly as Sam did. She craved it. His arm was around her shoulders and she received plenty of curious looks and speculative glances.

This kind of connection also terrified her. Music had always been her touchstone and she wouldn't—couldn't—allow herself to need anything else. It was her life's work and she wanted no other ties. Ties that bind, ties that would require her to expose her heart, ties that would require her to keep Sam's heart safe. She wasn't up to that task. She didn't want him to love her.

It all came down to a choice. Her gran had chosen love and her mother had chosen music above all else, even her daughter. And that hurt more than Jenna would ever let her mother see. She would be strong and untouchable, not responsible for anyone else's happiness.

She moved out from under Sam's arm and smiled at him. "I hate to be a killjoy, but do you think you'll be much longer? I should really practice."

Sam straightened and nodded. "Right. Gotta get along." He tipped his hat and went into the feed store. Jenna headed back to the truck, unsettled about her tumbled, jumbled feelings for Sam, the land, and this slice of small-town life. As she pulled open the truck's door, Sam came out of the feed store, a small bag in his hand. He smiled at her. As he came up alongside her, a man called his name and Sam turned to speak with him.

Jenna was struck by the strength of his profile. Clean, hard lines, his nose straight and fine, his chin strong and solid, his jaw like granite. When he turned to include her in the introductions, his eyes were deep, mesmerizingly blue. Honest, rough-hewn features gnawed at her composure in a way no others had before. He took off his hat, toying with the band. She quelled an urge to run her fingers through his thick hair and smooth it off his forehead. She turned away to keep from falling headfirst into the pulling effect of his eyes.

"Hey, Sam," the man said as they shook hands. "Been meaning to give you a call. I wanted to come and take a look at your stock of quarter horses. Millie needs a good barrel racer."

"I saw where she won the junior competition. That's impressive, Mike."

The man's voice was full of pride when he spoke. "She's a pistol, my Millie. Seems like she's twelve going on thirty and not one cowardly bone in her body. Keep trying to talk her out of rodeoing. Plumb near stops my heart to think of her on some mean ol' bull. Barrel racing is safer."

"Sure is. But what about the horse she rode in the competition?"

"Pulled a tendon and, I have to be honest, he's already peaked. She won by a tight margin and used most of her skill. I want her on a better horse, one of yours."

"My horses can hold their own."

The man turned to Jenna and huffed. "Can you believe this guy? Acting as if his animals are just *no slouches* in the competition business. I heard that Jigsaw's progeny Jigsaw's Puzzle won the roping competitions across the board. Hell, ever since Tuff McGee won the roping title on the circuit, riding Jigsaw's Puzzle, roper enthusiasts have been knocking down your door for Jigsaw's foals. Your daddy would be proud."

Jenna saw something in Sam she hadn't seen before. It was a quiet glow of satisfaction. She saw something else, too. A shadow of sadness streaked across his eyes very briefly before he looked down.

"Circuit?" Jenna echoed. "Rodeo?"

"Calf-roping competitions," Mike said. "What do you have here, Sam? A greenhorn?"

"She does all right for a greenhorn. Sorry, this is Jenna Sinclair."

"Ah, the fiddler. Heard she was staying with you."

"I'm ignorant of roping competitions and horse breeding, I'm afraid. I hope you won't hold that against me."

"Naw," he said, shaking her hand. "To each their own, I always say. Besides, I heard you play a mean piece on your instrument."

"Perhaps you'd like to attend my concert tomorrow night. The proceeds go to charity."

"It's a good cause. We'll be there."

Mike and Sam talked for a few more minutes about when he would come to the ranch and scope out a barrel racer for his daughter, then he left. Sam and

Jenna climbed into the truck and were once again on their way back to the ranch.

"Sam..."

His shoulders tensed and he turned to look at her, sadness returning to his eyes.

"Hmm?"

"Your father wasn't too keen on you raising horses, was he?"

"Not exactly."

"What do you mean?"

"My dad was not capable of helping me with the horses and said it was too much for him. The cattle were enough."

"That's why you left at eighteen?"

"Yes. I was angry and frustrated. Beef prices weren't as good as they had been in the past. I argued that we needed to diversify, but my father was a true rancher and man of the land."

"You said you came back because of your dad's health. It was more than his heart."

"It was more," he said, taking a deep breath and letting it out. "My father had a drinking problem. He had a lot of tragedy in his life. My older brother was stillborn and my mother died shortly after I was born. He never got over their deaths."

"And you got lost somewhere along the way?"

"Sort of. Tooter picked up the slack that my father's drinking caused."

"He's the one who taught you everything you know."

"He was like a father to me."

"He saved the ranch?"

"He saved my inheritance and my father's pride. He covered for my father, sobered him up and made sure he ate. Tooter worked hard. He believed in the breeding program and helped me every step of the way."

"Just like my gran nurtured and supported me." She thought about the connection before continuing.

"I guess Jigsaw had something to do with building your reputation, as well," Jenna asked, wanting to understand how the horse played an important role in Sam's life.

"The first time I saw that horse, I knew. He wasn't much to look at, but I could see he had heart. He was championship material. I took a chance on him and he didn't let me down."

Jenna's heart twisted in her chest. Sam would be relentless if he truly believed in something. It was no wonder he had made a success out of the Wildcatter, while his dad just eked out a living.

"Jigsaw's Pride was the first foal. I almost broke down and cried when she was born. I could see my future in her soft brown eyes. She's never let me down, either."

Jenna reached over and slid her hand against the skin of Sam's neck, needing the contact.

When they pulled up to the ranch, Tooter was standing on the front porch. As soon as Sam turned the ignition off on the truck, Tooter was at his window. Sam opened the door and stepped outside. Jenna came around the front of the truck and caught the tail end of Tooter's words.

"...been acting funny all day. I tried your cell, but you didn't answer."

"I was at the feed store." Sam was already heading for the foaling barn at a brisk walk, with Tooter running to catch up. It was obvious to Jenna that the horse requiring attention must be very important to Sam.

"I hope it's okay," Jenna called after him.

He stopped and turned. "Thanks," he said, and resumed his quick pace to the barn.

Jenna entered the house and stood for a moment in the foyer. Her stomach grumbled for lunch, but she ignored it and looked down the hall that would lead her to Sam's office and the diary.

She'd neglected her mission, pure and simple. She'd gotten caught up in Sam's blue eyes and his strong, clever hands. She was thinking dangerous thoughts about permanence and stability. Her life wasn't about that. It was about keeping up the pace and about freedom. It was about never letting anyone close enough, so that she'd never be in a position to have to make a choice.

One minute she was standing in the foyer and the next she was racing to the office. She had to find the diary. She had to. But when she got there, she pulled up short. Cal was at a filing cabinet with papers in his hands.

He turned to look at her as she stood breathless in the doorway.

"Did you need something, ma'am?" he asked.

"No. I'm sorry to bother you." She walked briskly away and emerged near the dining room. She quickly made her way to the living room and then the stairs. Maria was coming out of Sam's room with an armload of wash.

"Oh, you and Sam are home. Can I get you some lunch?" she asked as Jenna climbed the stairs.

"Sure. I'm not sure when Sam can eat. He's in the barn. I think it might be Jigsaw's Pride."

"Is there trouble?" Maria looked alarmed and moved over to the laundry basket near the top of the stairs and dropped the clothes in.

"I'm not sure, but Sam was concerned. That mare is important to him."

Maria nodded as she walked down the stairs and Jenna followed. "They're all important to him, but Jigsaw's Pride is special."

Jenna followed Maria into the kitchen. Maria got the bread out of the bread box and walked over to the refrigerator. "So is Jigsaw—he's a world-class cutter. Sam doesn't have the time to compete, so my older boy Matthew does that for him."

"How did Sam get Jigsaw?"

"That's a sad story. Sam was driving over to town when he passed some rancher who was beating Jigsaw badly. Sam stopped him. He offered to buy the horse on the spot, even called Tooter to get a trailer over there so that they could take him right away.

"He was pitiful at first, malnourished and mean. Sam worked with that horse every day until he trusted Sam. He gentled that horse with sheer willpower. Sam's not one to give up easily."

"Sam told me he left because his father wasn't interested in the horse business."

"It's not a secret. Everyone on this ranch heard them arguing about it."

"Did you know him back then, Maria?"

Maria smiled, her eyes softening. "I've been cleaning and cooking for this ranch since I was eighteen. Met Red here. The Winchester men have been very good to us."

"You must have known about Sam's father."

"That boy had a tough childhood, but Tooter was there. Sam was a sweet little boy, a solid teenager, and a fine man. You'll find no finer. He was frustrated with his daddy. That's all. Maybe wanted to prove something to himself. All I know is that the moment his daddy got sick, he was back here every weekend when he wasn't on Ranger duty."

"He's lucky to have you and Tooter."

"We're lucky to have the chance to work for such a fine family."

Pure emotion filled her chest. It hurt to think about how different their childhoods had been. Hers had been graced with music and a close, loving relationship with her grandparents. Tempered with firm discipline and strict rules. All that she wanted was attainable. All she had to do was reach for it. Even fame.

Sam, on the other hand, had had to create his own stability, though the struggle had built his strong, unfailing character.

Maria finished with the sandwiches. She put a serving of potato salad and a pickle on each plate.

"I'll let Sam know that lunch is ready."

"Let me."

Jenna went out the back door and headed for the foaling barn. When she entered, she saw Tooter and Red standing next to a box stall. As she approached she could see Sam inside with a beautiful black mare, her stomach heavy with her young.

Sam was smoothing his big hands along her stomach and Jenna couldn't stop the memories of those hands moving over her body.

"How is she?" she asked.

All three men looked at her. Red smiled and made room for her at the stall door. Tooter scowled his usual scowl, but also made room for her.

Sam came to her, a smile on his face. "Looks like she's doing fine. Tooter's fussier than an ol' hen."

Tooter snorted and Red laughed.

"She'll probably drop late tonight," Sam said.

"She's beautiful."

"Mr. Winchester?"

Sam leaned over the stall door and called. "Over here, Cal."

Red's youngest son smiled at his dad as he walked over to the stall. "There's a Mr. Sawyer here to see you."

"That was today?" Sam said, taking off his hat and wiping at the sweat on his brow. "Shoot. Tell him I'll be right out."

"Red, go get Jigsaw's Little Challenge."

"Ah, Tooter, Sam don't need to work that horse for Sawyer to know he's getting a prime piece of horseflesh."

"I know that. I just like to show him off. Go get him."

Sam laughed as Red went out shaking his head, Tooter right alongside him. Jenna smiled at the flashing grins and natural swaggers of the two men. Sam came out of the stall and closed the door.

When they left the foaling barn, a man was walking up to them, led by Cal. He reached out his hand and shook Sam's with enthusiasm. "Now, before you get to thinking that your dates are off, I'm a week early. I'd like to start working him for a roping competition next month. I hope that's fine with you."

"No problem, Ty. Just head over to the corral and I'll be right there. Red's bringing Challenge."

He turned to Jenna. "I have to go up to the house to change my boots."

She nodded. "You going to use your new roping spurs?"

He smiled. "Yep. Why don't you head over to the corral, too?" He brushed the back of his hand across her cheek. "You're getting all that pale skin tanned. Looks good on you." He smiled and winked, walking away.

Jenna didn't realize, until he had disappeared into the house, that she had watched his progress until he was out of sight. She couldn't take her eyes from the fit of his jeans across his tight, well-formed butt, the movement of his thigh muscles, the easy roll of his hips. She turned away, more than a little shaken by the longing that surged inside her.

She went to the corral fence and stood next to two cowhands who had discovered Sam was going to work the horse.

"You ever seen a roping horse in action?"

Startled, Jenna turned to find Tooter standing beside her. He was staring off into the distance.

"No. I don't know a thing about roping or the rodeo. Total greenhorn."

"First off, the calf gets a running head start—up to twenty feet. The rope horse has to overtake him. The cowboy has two throws to snag the calf. Once the rope's on him, the rope horse will pull up sharply and tauten the rope. Pulls the critter off his feet so the cowboy can use his pigging string to tie three legs together. Success in roping depends on teamwork between a cowboy and his horse. A little luck don't hurt none, either."

"What's a pigging string?"

"Short piece of rope."

"Does Sam provide any other stock to the rodeo?"

"No. Only trained horses—ropers, racers and cutters. But Sam has always liked the drama of roping. Most exciting to watch if you ask me."

When Sam showed up at the corral, he was wearing spurs, the jingle setting off firecrackers inside her.

"Mr. Sawyer said he was here early. What did he mean by that?"

"A foal is put through his paces from birth. Can't take the saddle until he's three years old, due to soft bones. Sam's particular about Jigsaw's get. No one trains that stallion's offspring until Sam says so. Challenge is a four-year-old. He's ready to go now, but Sawyer contracted for the end of May," Tooter said.

"Will Sam have a hard time parting with him?" Jenna asked.

Tooter nodded.

Red had taken the horse into one of the big, long corrals. The man with him proceeded to unhook the gate and wait for Sam. Jenna picked a good spot at the fence so she wouldn't miss any of the action.

A bawling calf was led to the corral, brought to the farthest fence, then tied.

Sam walked up to the magnificent horse that waited quietly on the lead. He was a gorgeous golden-brown with a milk-chocolate-colored tail, mane and legs, small and well proportioned, with well-developed hindquarters and an elegant head.

As Sam swung into the saddle, the buckskin's ears came forward, his neck arched and he tracked the calf with his liquid brown eyes.

Sam put the pigging string between his teeth and picked up the rope looped around the saddle. Jenna could see that the end of the rope was tied around the saddle horn. Sam let out the coil. His big body was tense and alert, his eyes forward and the hat on his head pulled low. He nodded to the man with the calf. As soon as the animal was free from the rope, it ran.

When the calf was about twenty feet from the horse, the buckskin leaped from a standstill to a full-out gallop. His big hindquarters ate up the ground easily, gaining on the calf. Sam's heavily muscled thighs gripped the sides of the horse, the rope up over his head, spinning in what looked like an effortless action.

She was awed by his easy command. The way man and horse worked as one, each seeming to know without cues or sound what the other expected. They were fluid action, power, intelligence.

Sam threw the rope with a quick flick of his wrist and Jenna's breath caught at the beauty of perfect harmony. The rope dropped over the calf's neck and immediately, in a blur of motion, Sam dismounted on the gallop, as the horse braked to a spectacular stop. The rope drew taut and the calf was pulled from his feet. In moments, Sam had three of his legs tied. He walked back to the horse, who never once let the rope go slack, and mounted. As soon as Sam was in the saddle, the horse took a step forward. The calf was still tied.

Everything must have happened in about eight to ten seconds from start to finish.

And it struck Jenna hard to the heart that more than anything—more than the townspeople, more than the chores, more than even the bucking bronc—this was the essence of who Sam was, and how closely he identified who he was with what he did. He didn't live as a cowboy. He was a cowboy.

It was a revelation and made her realize that she wouldn't be the woman for him. He needed someone who understood this lifestyle and could help him, support him, be part of it. A woman born of the West, brought up on a ranch, knew the terms and how to do what was necessary.

Shaken, Jenna couldn't take her eyes from him as he sat on the horse watching one of the cowhands untie the prone calf and set him free. She tried to breathe around the tightness in her chest. She understood why the cowboy was such a powerful sexual symbol. He was simply too potent. Too overwhelmingly male.

Sawyer moved down the corral fence as Sam dismounted and led the horse.

"Yehaw," the visitor crowed. "That's a Jigsaw get all right."

"Do you always buy from Sam?" Jenna asked, her attention on Sam as he slid his hand over the buckskin in quiet praise.

"I wouldn't trust my horseflesh to anyone else. The man's a genius with anything on four legs."

Sam relinquished the buckskin to Red with a nod. Jenna could see the sweat beaded on Sam's brow as he removed his sweat-stained hat and wiped at his forehead.

Sam didn't use the gate but climbed the corral fence and landed next to Jenna and Ty. Tooter had disappeared.

She retreated as Ty and Sam began to talk about competitions and horseflesh. Retreated to the house, first stopping in the kitchen to collect her lunch, then on to her room, where she deliberately changed back into the clothes she'd brought with her. She knew where she belonged and it was most definitely not here and not with this man. The realization that she had the power to bring Sam to his knees shivered through her. Tempted, so tempted to use it to bind him to her, but what would that mean for him? In time, she was sure she could talk him into selling the ranch, leaving Savannah. She was that sure about her power over him. It was something her mother wouldn't hesitate to do.

For Jenna it would be the ultimate evil. Jenna swore vehemently to herself.

She was absolutely nothing like her mother.

She would never, never destroy Sam like that.

Never.

He was better off without her and any influence she had over him.

She picked up her violin and began to practice.

Jenna hadn't expected to fall in love with this kind of lifestyle. She hadn't expected to fall in love with the town of Savannah. There was a closeness that tugged at her heart, a warm, easy feeling that Jenna wanted to capture and hold in her heart. It was like drinking tea with her gran, walking in the moonlight with her gramps and having him name the stars for her. It was like home.

The more time she spent at the Wildcatter the less she wanted to leave.

But leave she must.

12

___

A KNOCK ON THE DOOR hours later made Jenna drop her bow from the strings of the gleaming violin.

"Come in."

Sam poked his head around the door. He was grimy and looked tired. "Sorry to disrupt you, but you wanted to check out the honky-tonk tonight. Still up for it?"

Jenna almost told him that she needed to continue to practice, but she couldn't help herself. She craved time with Sam, time that was quickly running out. "Yes, I would, but are you sure you can leave Jigsaw's Pride? You said she's going to drop her foal tonight."

"Late tonight. Trust me, but if it makes you feel better, I've told Tooter to call me on my cell if there's any problem."

"You look tired."

"Nothing that a shower and some time with you won't cure. I'd like to teach you how to Texas two-step. Gives me the chance to get my arms around you. I'll be ready shortly."

"I'll be waiting."

Jenna showered and put on a pair of the faded jeans she'd bought. She picked up one of the cotton shirts and toyed with the collar. With the devil inside her, she went to her suitcase and opened it. Inside was a black spaghetti-strap shirt that would hug her curves and probably drive Sam crazy. Grinning, she pulled the shirt on. She quickly braided her hair and went downstairs.

She walked through the living room and stopped short. Sam was already in the foyer. The chandelier shone on his sinfully dark hair. He was dressed in a red T-shirt that made his shoulders look impossibly broad. It was made of silky material that delineated his back muscles and biceps and tucked into a pair of sinfully tight black leather pants. She followed the line of his powerful legs down to his feet. *Red* boots. He was wearing red boots.

He shook Jake Stanton's hand, handed him a check, then opened the door for him. Looked like Sam's office was finished. When he turned around, his eyes moved over her. He whistled long and low. "Nice. I can see I'm going to have to keep you close tonight or some randy cowboy's going to steal you away."

She walked up to Sam and draped her arms around his neck, pressing her body against his, emotions and revelations making her voice uneven. "He'd have to kidnap me to get me away from you. And what about all the cowgirls who are going to take one look at you and swoon?"

He flashed her a grin. "I'll just step over them as I escort you onto the dance floor."

They laughed and she reached up and ruffled his hair. "You are bad."

His blue eyes locked with hers and for a moment

he forgot to breathe through the grip of his hunger for this one woman. He savored the fact that she wanted him as deeply as he wanted her. And he was well aware that time was running out and soon she'd be gone.

He closed off that thought, because he wasn't willing to think about her leaving him. He lifted her face with one hand on her delicate jawline and fixed his mouth to hers, first gently, then with more fervor, as if to prove that fact to himself.

Jenna responded by rubbing her lips against his, opening her mouth to close it over his lips in what seemed like a bittersweet kiss. Their tongues dueled intimately before Sam sent his deep into her mouth, an indication of what he wanted to do to her. Sam could feel the womanly curve of her hip pressed tightly against the hard ridge straining against his pants.

He broke the kiss before he entered the point of no return. "We'd better get going before I haul you back up the stairs and into my bed. Last night seems such a long time ago."

Jenna looked up at him and smiled. "Yes, it does."

When they were in the truck and cruising through the darkness, Jenna asked. "Is Jake finished with your office?"

"Yeah. He did a fine job."

"You'll get a chance to use that beautiful rolltop desk."

"It makes the paperwork almost bearable."

They pulled up to Windy Bill's Honky-Tonk and

Saloon. As they exited the truck, the throbbing beat of the bar's music filled the night air.

They entered the place and Sam paid the cover. As they moved inside, Sam could see numerous couples on the dance floor. The bar was huge because Billy had expanded a few years ago due to the large number of couples coming from Galveston and Houston to enjoy the dancing and electronic bull.

Sam greeted numerous people as he walked by the crowded tables and busy bar. He was gratified that a few people called out to Jenna, too.

"Would you like to sit at a table?"

"Sure."

They settled in and soon their waitress, Ann Louise, was sidling up to their table. She was a perky blond pixie with a big heart and a pleasant smile. "Hey, Sam, how's my old uncle Red doing? I haven't seen him in a week."

"He's full of cuss and fight as usual."

"Tell him I said hey, and I'll visit next week."

"Sure will."

Ann Louise's curious eyes fell on Jenna. "You that musician I've heard so much about? I heard you were staying with Sam."

Jenna smiled. "Yes, I am."

"Nice to meet you. I really hope you're enjoying your stay. It's an admirable thing you're doing playing your fiddle to help out with the hospital. Sam is really dedicated to it. So what can I get you?"

"Beer would be fine. Jenna?" He was dedicated to the hospital, a project that had brought Jenna here. She'd been generous with her time. Sam felt the same pang of loneliness when he thought of his empty house. He would really miss her.

"I'd like a beer, too," Jenna replied.

Ann Louise smiled and moved on to the next thirsty customer.

"Would you like to have your first lesson?"

Jenna gazed at the crowded dance floor and looked apprehensive.

"It's not really hard, Jenna. Come on. You can trust me," Sam said, taking her hand.

She stood and clasped his hand. He led her to the dance floor. "Follow me." He took her hand, arranging her into the classic waltzing position. "You'll be stepping back while I move toward you. It's a two-step and pretty simple. It's four steps to six beats of music like this." He demonstrated by moving his feet and Jenna backed up. "Slide along. Don't pick up your feet." She was getting into the rhythm. "That's it," Sam said as he moved with her around the floor. "Fast, fast, slow, hold."

They danced that song and then the next. Sam liked the feel of her in his arms. He could imagine them dancing like this every Saturday night.

"Sam, can we try that twirling thing everybody's doing?"

"Brave little greenhorn, aren't you."

"Yeah, I take the bull by the horns."

"When I twirl you, don't worry about getting back into my rhythm. The gentleman always follows the lady. So just start with the two-step when you come out of the spin. Are you ready?"

Jenna nodded her head and Sam began to spin her,

trying other moves like crossing her over and spinning her back. Jenna followed right along. She was laughing and having a good time. Her eyes sparkled.

His gut clenched. Maria had been telling him for years that he needed a woman. He couldn't argue with her. But he sure as hell didn't need *this* one. He could still feel the silk of her hair in his hands, could see the smoke of surprising desire in her eyes. He could hear the sharp intake of her breath as he'd held her in his arms, her laughing in the hay, her standing in front of him with whiskey sliding over her hot nipple.

He knew better. Tight jeans were never enough of an excuse to lose your sense of direction. And Sam had never had a doubt about the direction his life would take from the moment he'd heard his father was ill. He'd quit the Rangers without a backward glance and had gone home. Ranching was in his blood. He would never be able to give it up.

But as he moved with Jenna in his arms, he was tempted to tell her that she seemed to fit in here. It had surprised him how easily she'd moved through his world, charming the small-town community, eating at the diner and buying clothes at a store that certainly wasn't Neiman Marcus or Bloomingdale's.

She'd helped him with a newborn calf, ridden in the rain and spent the night in rough surroundings without a problem. She'd tumbled him into the hay without an ounce of squeamishness. Damn, he liked her. In fact, he felt even more than that. It was only Jenna Sinclair, with her hot eyes and her soft mouth, with her gut-wrenching fire of enthusiasm, who could break this man's heart if he let her.

The song ended, and breathless with the spinning and laughter, Jenna said, "I need a drink."

They settled at their table and Jenna took a few gulps of her beer. Sam eyed her and smiled.

"Not very ladylike, is it?" she said, and laughed as she licked foam from those luscious lips. Sam felt his groin tighten and forced his hormones to heel.

Someone yelled out, "Hey, fiddler. Why don't you give us a tune?"

Sam looked at Jenna and she looked at the band.

The man with the fiddle held it out to her. Jenna gave Sam a mischievous smile, got up and walked over to the stage. The bar quieted. It was the first time that had ever happened in noisy Windy Bill's. Jenna looked out on the crowd, leaned over and said something to the band members. Big grins broke out on their faces. She put the bow to the fiddle and started playing a resounding version of a popular country-dance number. Most of the couples got up to dance.

Sam couldn't take his eyes off Jenna as she dipped and swayed and thoroughly enjoyed the number. Jenna played the last few notes and everyone clapped.

Jenna walked back over to the table, grinning.

"Where did you learn that tune?"

"I had a teacher who believed that we should learn all types of music. I loved that song and played it over and over until I learned it. It really helped me to play classical music better."

She sat down and Sam's cell phone rang. He pulled it off his belt and answered, "Winchester."

It was the first time in Sam's life he'd ever heard Tooter panicked. His blood ran cold.

"Sam, I don't know how it happened, but Jigsaw's Pride is in trouble. I've already called the vet," Tooter said.

"We'll be right there."

JENNA STOOD at the window that overlooked the foaling barn and waited for news of the mare and foal. She was anxious. Very anxious, because Sam had looked so worried. It hit her in the truck how much he cared for the mare. Why not? It was Jigsaw's first offspring and Sam's first result from a horse he believed in. She remembered how he'd told her about crying when he'd gotten the first foal he'd ever bred. Though the mare had already given him seven sturdy foals, two fillies and five colts, Jenna knew he couldn't bear to lose the horse and her unborn foal.

It was driving her crazy. She wasn't accustomed to caring this much about anyone except her grandparents. She should be sleeping. She had a concert tomorrow, but she couldn't seem to rest. Her music just didn't seem as compelling in the face of this crisis.

She should be sensible.

Instead, she was fascinated. She was driven. She was—God help her—worried sick about Sam. She'd come here to the Wildcatter to retrieve her gran's diary. That was all. It had been a simple plan. Even now, when she could have gone down to that desk and searched through it, she just couldn't seem to do it. The guilt would be too much. It would seem like such a horrible betrayal of a man who'd been simply wonderful to her.

How could she enjoy such a small town? The hustle and bustle of New York seemed so far away. And having had a taste of a simpler life, she'd discovered she liked its rhythms and characters.

And she'd been able to concentrate on only one character. One rugged, enigmatic character with the most intriguing smile and a rigid code of the West she couldn't help but admire.

It should have been so easy.

Now it was a complicated mess.

Only two facts remained. She had to get the diary and she had to leave here. Yet the night passed and, as dawn's first light filtered over the quiet ranch, she turned away from the window, went out the door and down the stairs. But as she made her way to Sam's office, the front door opened. Sam stood there, seemingly struck dumb. He just stared at her as if his heart had been broken. Jenna knew immediately.

She went to him.

''We lost them both. The foal was stillborn and...'' The words jammed in his throat. He closed his eyes, the dark stubble emphasizing the hard set of his jaw. His immobility would have alarmed her if he hadn't been clasping her hand so tightly. The tangible feel of his skin against her own made her chest unutterably tight.

Jenna tugged him until he crossed over the threshold and stood in the foyer. ''Come with me, Sam.''

He followed her up the stairs to his bathroom. An uneasy tremble beat against her breastbone. She propped him against one wall. She could see clearly the fatigue on his face, the sense of loss in his eyes. Her vision blurring, Jenna turned on the tap and adjusted the water temperature until it was perfect. When she touched him, her chest grew tight at the way he was shaking. Quickly wiping away her tears, she slid her arm around his waist. "Come on, Sam," she whispered unevenly. "Let's get you into the shower and to bed."

For a moment, she thought he was going to protest. But he sighed unsteadily and straightened. With his cooperation, Jenna started to undress him, clenching her jaw against the tender feeling that sluiced through her. Once he was free of his boots, jeans, shirt and underwear, she helped him into the shower and quickly undressed herself.

He shuddered when she wrapped her arms around his waist and pushed him under the spray. She washed him with quick efficiency, lathering his hard, muscled body and enticing him to rinse. Soaping his hair, kneading his scalp with the pads of her fingertips trying to give him some small degree of comfort.

Once she got him wiped off, she took him to the bed, where he stretched out on his back, his arm across his eyes, his jaw taut.

He hadn't moved a muscle when Jenna came back from the bathroom, and he remained in the same position when she got into bed beside him. She slid her arm under his neck and gently drew his arm away from his eyes. "Let me hold you, Sam," she requested quietly.

He lay immobile for a minute, his breath slipping out of him in a shuddering whoosh. Turning into her arms, Sam changed position, slid his leg over hers, pulling her tight against him. Squeezing her eyes closed against the hard lump in her throat, she cradled his head against her breast and pressed her mouth to the top of his head. Jenna swallowed hard and draped the sheet over his shoulders, then began slowly kneading the heavy muscles of his back. Her physical comfort seemed to help him to settle down. The shaking stopped and he released another ragged sigh. He turned his face to her, his beard rasping against her skin. His weight grew heavy against her, and she hoped he'd fallen asleep, free from the loss he'd suffered, but he tightened his arm around her and spoke, his voice thick. "Thanks for being here."

She hugged him against her and blinked back the tears in her eyes. "You're welcome," she whispered unevenly.

In all the times she'd shared his bed, in all the different ways they had made love, that night she was suddenly intensely tuned to him—the soft way he breathed when he slept, the silk of his hair, the scent of his skin, the heat he radiated. She stayed alert hours after he'd fallen asleep, absorbing even the smallest detail, her chest so full of pain and guilt that she couldn't breathe at times. He slept a totally exhausted sleep, something so helpless in his quiet slumber that she felt the need to shield him.

She had never been the one to give anyone comfort. She'd always received it from her gran. It made her heart ache for a closer, more intimate connection with Sam. The thought also made her panic. She could easily get attached to these emotions he evoked in her. And she dreaded the loneliness she knew she would experience once she was back in New York.

He finally stirred in the early afternoon, the patter of rain on the roof invading their cocoon, broadcasting that there was a world outside of Sam's bedroom. One that had to be faced. He shifted beside her, his stubble abrading her skin when he turned his head, his breath warm against her neck as he breathed her name. He was still in the beginning stage of waking and the soft sound of her name did amazing things to her heart. She smoothed her hand through his hair, feeling a wealth of tenderness for him that made her chest tight.

He shifted his head, then with a sleepy caress, he curved his hand around her rib cage. Breathing deeply, he slid his arms around her and gathered her up in an enveloping embrace, then spoke, his voice gruff with sleep. "Jenna, you feel so good."

Easing past the aching fullness in her chest, she tightened her arms around him. "You feel pretty darn good yourself," she whispered unevenly.

She felt him swallow, and that one gesture ignited her heartfelt compassion. She clenched her jaw, cupping the side of his face. She tipped her head and pressed a kiss against his cheekbone. Sam turned his head and captured her mouth, taking it in a slow, lazy kiss that sent her pulse skittering. Releasing his breath in an unsteady sigh, he tightened his hold on her face and drew away.

Jenna studied his handsome face, close to tears for this man she hadn't known existed just a short week and a half ago.

Sam pulled her beneath him, his weight braced on his forearms as he pressed his body along her length.

His hand tangled in her hair, his hips flush with hers. He nudged her thighs apart with his knee and settled his legs between hers, his erection hard and hot between them. He tightened his hold, brushed a kiss against her neck and said, his voice rough with emotion and tenderness, "I need you, Jen."

Of all the things he could have said, that was the one thing she craved and feared.

He buried his face against her neck and Jenna felt his chest expand. Abruptly, everything changed. Her breath caught an immediate wild need for him, eclipsing everything, including her fear. Closing her eyes, she hung on to him, a heady weakness pulsing through her. On a soft moan of pleasure, she widened her knees.

"I want to be inside you, deep inside," Sam said.

Shaken to the core by the agony in his voice, her body primed for the feel of him, she rubbed her wet heat against him. "Yes," she whispered, her voice breaking from the intensity of her surging desire.

Sam roughly tightened his hold and made a low sound, and Jenna arched her back and lifted her pelvis. Sam went rigid in her arms, another low, ragged groan wrenched from him as he entered her in one thrust.

There was no room for tenderness or control. There was only room for exigency and a fever of need that coalesced into a driving hunger that consumed them, pushed them, drew them to the very edge of a poignant abyss; then Sam clutched her and drove into her one final time. The blackness exploded into splintering shards of silver. The paralyzing release took them both under.

Sam held her tightly in his arms. His body shuddered against hers, and Jenna clung to him, so shaken, so emotionally exposed that she felt stripped inside. It took a long time for all that emotional turmoil to settle, and the first things she was aware of were how close she was to crying and how securely he was holding her. She released some of what she was feeling by releasing the air in her lungs, then she cupped the back of his head and hugged him hard.

Sam inhaled unevenly, then turned his head and kissed her on the curve of her neck. Jenna could feel his heart hammering against hers. "Are you all right?" he whispered, his voice rough with emotion.

She nodded, burying her face against his neck. She waited for the pressure to ease in her chest. "Are you?"

Drawing one arm from under her, he braced his weight on it and looked down at her. With the dark stubble shadowing his strong jaw, his heavy-lidded eyes and his tousled hair, he looked dark and dangerous and very male. He gave her a slow smile, a trace of amusement in his eyes. "I'm fine."

Jenna knew he was trying to lighten the mood, and it touched her deeply. She slid her hand up his neck and kissed him back, trying to be as emotionally honest as she could be under the circumstances. Holding her still, Sam eased away, then sighed and raised his head, his eyes dark and somber as he gazed down at her. Jenna tried to ease the contraction in her throat, then spoke, her voice unsteady. "I'm glad I came here, Sam."

He shifted his gaze as he drew his thumb across her mouth, and she saw the muscles in his jaw bunch. He met her eyes and the directness in his made her throat contract even more. "So am I," he answered. "So am I." He leaned down and kissed her again, then carefully withdrew from her. Using his arm as leverage, he lifted himself off her, then stretched out on his back and reached for her.

Jenna lay with her head on his shoulder and her knee tucked between his, the weight of his arm across her back holding her securely against him. She stared into the gray gloom, her hand splayed against his chest, listening to the counterpoint of his heartbeat and the rain on the roof, savoring the shared silence. Sam sighed and covered her hand with his, and Jenna shifted her head a fraction of an inch. "What are you thinking about?"

He sighed again and shook his head. "Wondering if I could have done anything to save her or if I'm just torturing myself."

He rubbed his thumb across her palm and then shook his head again. "Probably just torturing myself."

Jenna couldn't possibly understand what he was feeling. "What did the vet say?"

"That there wasn't anything I could have done differently. It was just one of those things. The foal was too big. It tore something inside her and we couldn't stop the bleeding."

"I'm so sorry, Sam."

He smoothed his hand across the swell of her hips, his expression sober. "I know you are and I appreciate it. It's getting late and you have a concert tonight. I'm sure you need to practice."

"I wish I could lie here with you."

A sensual gleam appeared in his gaze. He ran one finger back and forth across her bottom lip, his touch erotic and sensitizing. "I wish you could, too."

She stared at him and gave him a slow smile. "I know most of the music I'm going to play later."

He laughed and dragged her on top of him. He looked at her, pure male mischief sparkling in his eyes. "Is that so?" He shifted beneath her, then drew her head down and licked her bottom lip, murmuring, "Shoot, what can we do to take up the boring slack?"

Laughing at his naughtiness, Jenna replied, "I'm sure if we put our heads together, we can think of something."

Later, she found that she did have time to practice and did so up until they had to head to the Tannenbaum theater. The concert went off without a hitch, but Jenna was surprised to see so many of the Savannah natives peppering the audience. They clapped loud and long and she gave two encores. When she returned to her dressing room, she was shocked to find it full of flowers from so many townspeople.

The reception she found staid and, eventually she coaxed Sam to take her back to the honky-tonk. When they entered in their finery, everyone hooted and hollered, and teased them.

Jenna had the time of her life.

It wasn't until she was back in her bedroom that

the first tentacle of panic uncurled in her belly. Panic and guilt. She didn't know how it could work between them. She didn't know how to climb over the mountain of self-doubt. And she didn't know how she would survive when she walked out of his life.

It was then that she decided to search the desk, even as the feelings tormented her. She was leaving tomorrow. She had to leave tomorrow. She couldn't stay here.

She rushed out of her room and headed straight for Sam's office. Once there, she began to systematically go through the desk, but there was no diary. No jewelry. She clutched at her throat. He must have found them. He must have them.

She'd been a fool.

"What the hell do you think you're doing?"

She turned at the sound of Sam's voice.

"I want my grandmother's diary."

13

"WHAT DIARY?" Sam said, the confusion very clear on his face.

She held his gaze, searching his eyes. "Like you said, you bought this desk at auction. It should never have left my gran's house." Jenna was starting to get a bad feeling about this, her stomach churned.

Sam was clearly astonished. "This was your grandmother's desk?"

Jenna nervously moistened her lips. "The diary has to be in here. The other two desks were empty."

"You came here because of this desk, not for the hospital charity?" Now he sounded hurt. His eyes filled with disappointment and shock. "You lied to me?"

"Yes. Sam, it's extremely important that you give the diary to me. They hold scandalous information and I can't let that get out. I promised my gran. I also request that you return the jewelry to me."

His chin lifted and his eyes blazed. "I don't have your grandmother's diary or any jewelry. You came here for nothing."

Jenna felt battered by his words, his emotions, his power. She felt exposed and vulnerable and very guilty. She struggled to stand her ground, to keep her head up, to pull words free of the whirling emotions his facing her had unleashed. It wasn't until this very moment that she realized that she'd done this on purpose. She knew Sam couldn't have taken the diary. She knew it, yet she'd wanted to destroy his feelings for her. It was for the best. He should dislike her. It would be easier for him.

He turned and walked out of the room, and it wasn't until Jenna heard the front door slam that she snapped out of her lethargy. "Sam," she called, her voice now very small.

She rushed out of his office into the hall to the front door. She saw his retreating back in the downpour. Heedless of the rain, she bolted off the porch after him.

Sam felt as if his heart had been torn out of his chest. She was here on a pretense of helping them with the charity, of gaining the *real ranch experience*. It was all over some diary and jewelry she thought he'd stolen from her.

How could she think that of him? How could she accuse him of that? If he'd found something in that old desk, he would have done everything in his power to give it back to its owner. The pain raked at him, her distrust more wounding than the fact that she was here under false pretenses. She should have known that. She should have known him.

"Sam!"

He stopped and turned as Jenna raced against the powerful wind and rain. She barreled into him and caught him off guard and they tumbled down the embankment, landing in the hollow of the hill, shielded from the house and the barns.

She was on top of him, their legs entwined, her wet hair across his face.

Jenna looked down at him, her eyes bruised and haunted and the wrenching vulnerability on her face made his chest burn. All she was wearing was the yellow nightgown with thin straps. The color of the material made her skin glow. The silk garment was soaked and he could clearly see her dusky nipples through the transparent material, as well as the rest of her glorious body. She was so beautiful his body leaped in reaction, and she was so unsure of herself that his throat ached. His gaze moved down her slender torso, curving narrow at the waist, her hips round and firm, and her long legs smooth and tanned.

He knew then that if he had to do without her, his life would be one big empty joke. His eyes traveled back up, centering on her breasts and the exposed nipples. They hardened under his gaze. He reached out, curled his fingers around the strap and pulled her roughly into his arms. "Sam," she pleaded. "Sam."

Her eyes traveled over him in a hungry, desperate slide and he felt himself respond to the need on her face.

"Sam," she whispered, and he had to strain to hear her over the pounding rain. Then her voice strengthened and her chest heaved with the power of her trapped emotions. "I'm sorry. So sorry."

Something hard and painful eased inside him, relief rushing through him like a soothing caress. "I know," he said.

"There were three desks. My rotten uncle sold them. I was afraid that you wouldn't understand and you'd keep the diary. I know now that you couldn't possibly do that. You'd never do that."

"No. I'd never do that." The pain eased in his chest with her heartfelt admission.

His head rose off the ground. "Sam," she begged.

He looked up at her. "Jenna, I love you." His mouth closed over her nipple and she arched wantonly into the heat of him. She moaned his name again; the sound of it reverberated against the hills enclosing them, throwing his name back at them like an aching echo of wrenching need.

He sucked hard and she cried out and he felt satisfaction turn from an ember into a full, raging conflagration of hunger.

His hands moved up her arms, the pounding rain making her skin feel erotic and smooth to his touch. He reached for one strap and pulled it off her shoulder, then the other. He exposed her breasts to his eyes, his hand cupping the plump globes. His hands looked huge against the smallness of her exquisite body. The sight was so arousing that he hardened with painful desire. He growled low in his throat and pushed her onto her back, the gown caught between them, her upper body totally exposed to his hungry gaze. He took each nipple in turn. He moved with wild abandon against her, unable to stop the frenzy of powerful need that drove him.

Jenna reached down and freed him. His erection bracketed between her hand and the silk. Every time he moved his hips in an uncontrollable thrust, he encountered the erotic slide of the silk against his hardness.

Never in his life had he felt so out of control. The taste of her was like ambrosia, intoxicating until he felt as if the very life of her was in his blood, pumping through his heart and pulsing in every cell of his body. He couldn't get enough of her, felt as if he'd waited his whole life to have her like this.

His mouth moved up her body to her succulent lips and he took the wet, satiny skin with a harsh demand, bordering on brutality. Jenna was not passive, and returned his kiss with just as much force, just as much demand. She knew what she wanted and Sam almost howled out loud because it was him.

She wanted him.

The nagging concerns, the terrible revelations, the betrayal faded into the world beyond the hill. There was nothing but them, nothing but the driving need that wouldn't let them rest until it was met.

His hands roamed her body in feverish activity and where it met silk, he pushed the material away from her only to encounter silkier skin beneath.

Her hands roamed over the hard muscles of his back, through the strands of his hair, and kneaded his powerful shoulders. Where she touched, there was tingling fire that caused him to close his eyes. Having her hands on him threatened what precious little control he had left.

His hands slid down the curve of her bottom, raising her leg, lifting her and pressing her into the part of him that ached for her the most. The harsh cry that came from her made him wild with need. He pressed her back, her legs and arms wrapped around him. The softness, the wetness of her felt delicious against him. Woman, warm, his, and his mind reeled with the fact that it was Jenna who clung to him with such abandon.

He'd never loved anyone more, never craved anyone more, couldn't ever see himself with anyone but Jenna.

The sounds of their lovemaking mingled with the heavy sound of the rain. He clasped her tighter to him and with a bucking thrust, entered her deeply. Jenna arched into him, her nails digging into his back. She cried his name in a pleasure-soaked voice. The fire of his need for her savaged him and he moved against her mindlessly, the force driving him.

She matched him in that savage moment of unleashed passion. A passion buried deep, denied after so many years, broke free and left them both shaking with the intensity of their feelings.

His body seemed beyond him. There was only the driving need to claim her, make her unequivocally his. His breathing was thready as he pulled her harder against him and she was close to the edge. He endeavored to push her over and, when she froze, an amazed look came over her face. Sam watched her slide into and relish the explosion of pleasure that swamped her and her senses.

It was the final push to his highly aroused body. He followed her into the blast, and he knew it struck at him just as sharply.

''Jenna.'' His voice was rough, hoarse, full of his need for her. At the sound of her name, she clutched him tight and held on to him. In the aftermath of the climax, he felt her whole body shaking. When he raised his face, she was sobbing quietly, tears streaming down her face.

"I love you, Jenna."

"No. Don't say that. Don't."

"I have to. I want you to stay here. We can work it out. I know it."

"I'm sorry about everything," she said. She shook her head and buried her face in his neck and cried even harder. "Oh, Sam," she said in a broken voice. "I'm so sorry I hurt you. I wanted to protect you. I'd have to choose and I can't. I love my music too much. I can't give it up, not even for you. Tell me you understand, Sam. You need a woman who will be a true rancher's wife and stand by you. You have to know that."

"I understand how you feel about your music. I'm not asking you to change your whole life to stay here," he said, his own voice thick, because he did understand. He understood too well. "I'm only asking for a balance, Jenna. I'm not asking you to choose."

She raised her head, her stricken eyes causing painful damage to his heart. "I can't," she cried, her voice so unsteady, he could barely hear her. "It wouldn't work. There is no balance for me. There's only my music. It's what my father asked my mother to do, and she couldn't do it. Find yourself a woman who wants what you want, Sam. I'm not the right woman for you."

"Dammit, Jenna," Sam protested. "So that's it.

You're leaving and there's nothing I can say to make you stay.''

''Nothing.'' She took a shaky breath, as if bracing herself. Then she continued, her voice only slightly stronger. ''I have to leave tomorrow like I promised my agent. I have a tour to finish. I guess the diary must be lost.''

Clenching and unclenching his jaw, he reached down deep for control. He realized that he truly didn't blame her. He drew her tight against his body. The rain pounded against his skin as he held Jenna, a cold, hollow feeling unfolding inside of him. This was only the eye of the storm. The other half was coming and it would be more vicious and uncompromising than what had preceded it.

Even though they'd come to an understanding, she was slipping away from him and he wondered how he could survive losing Jenna.

THE PLANE TOOK OFF into the morning sky. Tooter, of all people, had driven her to the airport and Jenna couldn't face him. His silence had been like a lash against her heart.

When he dropped her at the terminal, all he said was, ''Have a safe trip.'' Then he was gone. With a heavy heart, she had made her way to the ticket counter and then, when they called for boarding, she'd gotten on the plane.

When the seat belt sign went off, Jenna reached down and took the red diary out of her briefcase. She flipped to the page where she'd left off.

Afterward I lay in his arms, spent, satisfied and determined to see this man again. I couldn't imagine being without him, but the reality was that I had to go back to New York and he would stay in Oahu.

As the day approached for me to leave, I got more distraught and couldn't bear it. When he came to see me, I told him that I loved him. He was so very sweet as he took my hand and told me that he loved me, too. It was the most wonderful, glorious moment of my life. I laughed and fell into his arms.

We spent the day together. His love intensified the passion, made it fuller and richer and achingly sweet. It was all that I wanted, dreamed of.

I learned a valuable lesson from that navy officer. I learned that love was missing from the encounters. That's why they were so empty for me. Before I left, he gifted me with a locket—a simple gold locket.

We wrote to each other every day and the moment he got out of the navy, we were wed.

His name is Daniel Chandler and I love him with every fiber of my being. My quest has ended and so has my diary.

The navy officer had been her grandfather and the locket that Jenna now wore around her throat had been the very one her grandfather had given her grandmother. Tears streamed down Jenna's cheeks as she closed the book that had taught her so much. She touched the locket and pried open the edges. Inside was an inscription. Thanks for Taking A Risk on Me. All My Love, Daniel.

Jenna squeezed her eyes closed, wishing she had the courage to let Sam take a risk on her.

14

JENNA RUBBED at the sore spot just below her hairline. The rest of the tour had been long and arduous. It was now early October and her last scheduled concert was at the end of the month. There was a definite chill in the air. She was far removed from the balmy two weeks in April she'd spent at Sam's ranch.

She gazed out the window of her agent's apartment and longed for grassy meadows and grazing longhorns, gamboling foals and their ever-patient mothers.

Longed for the feel of Sam's hands on her, making her drown in sensation and need. She closed her eyes.

She had felt isolated when she'd first stepped foot on the ranch. Isolated because of its alienness. At first the intense quiet had unnerved her.

But she soon realized that it didn't matter where she was. She would always feel lonely. The kind of loneliness that felt the same whether you were sitting silently in a wide-open meadow, or a two-bedroom apartment in the middle of the busiest city on earth.

Jenna was lonely. Desperately and definitely, isolated at first by her upbringing and then by her sudden, surprising fame.

"You must be tired," Sarah said as she handed Jenna a cup of coffee.

"That's an understatement." Jenna sipped the coffee, enjoying the warm liquid as it traveled down her throat.

"You miss him."

"You know me too well, Sarah. It's scary."

"Why don't you call him?"

"I'm too busy touring. My music comes first."

"Jenna, don't make any rash decisions. Maybe you could work it out with him."

"I'm not being rash. I can't make a commitment to Sam. I can't hurt him like my mother hurt my father."

"Are you sure? You're not your mother."

"I'm afraid to try. I couldn't bear it if I failed him." When Jenna had attended Julliard, no one had come forward to get to know her. They'd stared at her and talked at her, but never to her. Then the touring began and Jenna had been far from New York. She'd traveled from one city to another in hopes of finding some kind of place she could feel comfortable.

Besides Gran, being at the ranch with Sam was the closest she'd ever felt to that. No one cared who she was or what the glittering world of music thought about her. The people of Savannah had embraced her as easily as they embraced anyone. Maria had offered coffee and conversation, Lurleen warmth and friendship, and Sam...Sam offered something even a famous violinist couldn't put to music. A glittering edginess, a keen physical responsiveness, a gnawing deep inside where the pain of her mother's abandonment sat, memories of her father's loneliness and heartache lived, and all the dreams Jenna still dreamed.

"Besides, I've burned my bridges there. I told him my music was more important. I deceived him and seduced him." Sam Winchester pulled at her in a way no one and nothing had in her life. He had what her gran would call "tough character." Sam shadowed her dreams and haunted her days with the feel of his callused hand against her cheek, the steel of his eyes and the depth of his heart.

And yet, hidden where no one who knew Sam thought to look lay ghosts that echoed Jenna's. Ghosts of not having anyone close, of frustration and need. Behind that cowboy charm, behind the enigmatic sex symbol, hidden deep inside him was a hunger that scared her right down to her toes, because it was a hunger that made hers pale in comparison.

"I think you should plan a trip back to Savannah and give it a try."

Jenna shook her head sadly. "No, Sarah. What I have now is all that I'll ever have. I made my choice and it's music."

After leaving Sarah's office, Jenna felt compelled to stop at her gran's gravesite. She hadn't been there since her gran's funeral. The moon was yellow and full, the stars paying homage to its golden glow.

She still carried around the diary that her gran had given her. "I read the diary like you asked, but the magic you found with Gramps won't work for me, Gran."

She heard her gran's voice in her head as if she

was standing beside her now playing the devil's advocate.

Yes, it will. Reach for it.

Jenna closed her eyes and memories flooded back to her about how beautifully her gran and gramps had compromised. They had a wonderful balance because each one gave to the other.

You can have the same balance. Reach for it.

The thought burst on her like a supernova over her head. Her gran was right. Jenna suddenly knew that she did have the capacity to do that. It was her mother who didn't. Gran had been the perfect role model. She had taught Jenna about love.

Do you love him, Jenna?

"Yes," she whispered on the cold night air. "I do love him with all my heart."

What has that taught you?

"Sam's love for me taught me that there is more to life than my music. Happy?" she said to the gravestone. "I've always had my music to bolster me and I'm beginning to realize that in life there is so much more. More than I could possibly have imagined."

In Sam's touch, in the depth of his eyes, in the strength of his heart was more than music, more than sex—it was life. It was living and being loved. Her words rasped out, tears stinging her eyes. "It was everything."

STARS PEPPERED the heavens with a diamond-bright light, the moon yellow in the inky black sky. A strong wind wove through the cedars, rustling the dry leaves.

He could hear the lowing of the longhorns. On the cool night air, owls hooted and hunted.

Music of the plain, rich in melody, with a song that tore at Sam's heart.

He pushed away from the barn door to go into the house to rest, but probably not to sleep. His tempered heart and unyielding thoughts would not allow it. He closed his eyes against the pressure in his chest. He didn't have to look to the corral, where hollow purple shadows gathered in the first of night. He could still feel her tingling in his palms, radiating heat through every pore in his body, thundering through his beating heart, creating devastating pressure in his groin. His chest rose on a sharp ache, a raw longing. A hopeless need.

"Jenna."

The wind winnowed through his hair, catching her name and drawing it into the night, taking it to the glittering stars. He wondered where she was and if she looked at the same twinkling black sky.

LATER, HE TOSSED and turned. And when morning came, Sam's restless heart still plagued him. He went to the barn and headed for the tack room. Mending tack was all he was good for today.

"We've certainly gotten a lot of work done since that city slicker went home."

Sam turned to see Tooter standing at the tack room door.

"Tooter. I'm not in the mood," Sam answered, his tone flat. He took two leather screws out of a headstall, setting them on his workbench.

Tooter shifted, leaning his small bulk against the door, crossing his arms over his chest. It didn't look like Tooter had any plans of heeding the warning in Sam's voice.

"You're not sorry to see her go. Too much like that female you married," he snorted.

Sam threw the broken cheek strap into a plastic bin below the workbench. "She wasn't anything like Tiffany!" Sam bellowed.

"She didn't have the right duds." Tooter scratched at the gray stubble on his face.

"She adapted." Sam grabbed a replacement strap and fit it into place, testing the fit. "At least she was open to different clothes and riding. She even helped me deliver longhorn twins."

"But she didn't have staying power."

Those words unleashed the anger that had been simmering in Sam all along. He shoved the headstall away from him. The piece of leather slid off the workbench and hit the floor. Sam rose and walked over to Tooter. "She just didn't realize how much strength she has or how good we'd be together. We could make it work!"

Tooter blinked at Sam a couple of times and then said quietly, "Don't tell me. Try telling her. Moping about the place ain't going to get her back."

Sam stepped back and studied Tooter for a moment. Tooter sighed heavily. "Go after her, boy."

"Why, you old…"

"Careful, son. Have respect for your elders."

Why couldn't he and Jenna try? He knew that he could convince her. He loved her and wanted her back. When a Texas Ranger, former or otherwise, makes a decision, nothing can stand in his way, not even his stupid pride or Jenna's obvious fear of loving him.

A big smile pulled at Sam's mouth and lit up his eyes. "Looks like I have some airline reservations to make."

Tooter smiled too and clapped Sam on the back. "I'll drive you to the airport."

THE WALLS OF CARNEGIE HALL reverberated with audience applause. They made her come back for three encores. She waited until the clapping ceased. Stepping up to the microphone, she said, "Thank you, ladies and gentlemen. I can't tell you how wonderful it's been to perform for you, but I've decided that this will be my last tour for a while."

A murmur went through the crowd. "I'm going to semiretire."

Somebody stood up and began to clap and, before Jenna knew it, they were all on their feet clapping enthusiastically. Tears stung her eyes and she bowed.

Jenna walked to the edge of the stage and peered into the crowd. A man caught her eye—he looked so achingly familiar that her heart lurched into her throat.

She left the stage, but waited and watched as the crowd wandered out of the hall, yet that one man moved away from the rest and came down the aisle instead.

Jenna bit her lip to keep herself from leaping forward. Sam walked toward the stage and moved up the stairs. He was dressed all in black from his booted feet to the Stetson on his head.

He reached out his hand and in it was a ring box. ''Are you crazy?'' Jenna asked.

''Crazy about you.''

She laughed full and throaty. Very deliberately she held out her violin. ''Could you hold this for me?''

Sam didn't hesitate. He took the instrument. His smile hurt her heart. She traded him for the ring box and opened it. The diamond flashed under the dazzling houselights.

''Marry me, Jenna. I know we can make it work. I love you.''

''My mother was very cruel to my father because music was all that she cared about. I was afraid that I would do that to you.'' She looked up from the breathtaking diamond to the quiet, sweet love in Sam's eyes. ''I used the refusal to give up my music as a barrier between us, because I was afraid of letting you take a risk with your heart.''

''And now.''

''I want to move to your Texas ranch and settle down in one place, because I can't think of anywhere on earth I'd rather be than with you.''

''Jenna, what about your music?''

''I'm sure the college would consider giving me a teaching position. I only plan on doing select concerts and I hear Houston has a wonderful symphony orchestra.''

He held the violin tight to his chest. With his free hand, he reached out. Jenna took the ring out of the box and placed it on her left ring finger. Then she placed her hand into Sam's. She could feel the heat of him seeping into her, warming her all the way to her heart.

She threw her arms around his neck and kissed him.

"Sam?"

"Yeah."

"I love you."

"Well, isn't that convenient, sugar, because I love the hell out of you."

Jenna laughed softly and led him to her dressing room for her things. As they descended the stairs outside the complex, Jenna saw the horse-drawn carriage waiting at the curb.

She turned to Sam. "What a beautiful idea," she breathed, kissing his mouth. Everyone on the stairs of Carnegie Hall clapped as Jenna, holding tight to Sam's hand while he assisted her into the carriage, beamed with love and happiness.

Softly, she whispered into the dark night as Sam settled next to her, "Thanks, Gran."

ONCE THE CARRIAGE ride ended in Central Park, Jenna and Sam had taken a cab to her apartment. He had explored every inch of the two-bedroom place while she put her things away.

"This is a gorgeous desk."

At his words something inside her clicked. "Desk?"

"This is a French mahogany writing desk," Sam said.

Jenna eyed the table that held her numerous plants.

"I've had this table for years. My gran gave it to me."

She looked at him, a gleam in her eye. "I naturally assumed that when my gran referred to a desk, she was talking about one of the desks she kept in her attic."

They immediately began to search the desk. As Jenna did so, her hands came up against something that sounded hollow. She rapped a couple of times and then, finally, crawled under the desk. A panel slid away from a small compartment. Items fell into her waiting hands. A leather-bound book and a cloth-wrapped bundle.

Jenna crawled out from under the desk. Slowly, she unrolled the cloth and found jewel-encrusted nipple rings from an Egyptian prince, a fine waist chain from a French courtesan, and a very suggestive ivory necklace from a very helpful little hula dancer.

Jenna looked at Sam and opened the diary. "Wow, my gran was some wild woman. I think we should read this together."

Sam picked up the gold waist chain and wrapped it around her midriff. As their eyes met, Jenna began to clear the plants from the writing desk. She turned to Sam and smiled.

Her heart was full, her life bright and beautiful ahead of her, filled with music, love and Sam. She reached out and snagged a handful of his shirt. She leaned back onto the desk, deliberately drawing him between her legs. Grasping the shirttails, one in each fist, she jerked upward and opened the black denim shirt from his naval to his throat. The snaps made a clicking sound as they popped open.

Sam's eyes began to glow. Sweet, sweet man.

She surged forward and kissed the strong column of his throat, gliding her tongue along his collarbone.

"So, cowboy, have you ever done it on a desk?"

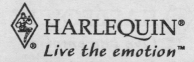

*They're strong, they're sexy, they're not afraid to use
the assets Mother Nature gave them....*

Venus Messina is...

#916 WICKED & WILLING
by Leslie Kelly
February 2003

Sydney Colburn is...

#920 BRAZEN & BURNING
by Julie Elizabeth Leto
March 2003

Nicole Bennett is...

#924 RED-HOT & RECKLESS
by Tori Carrington
April 2003

The Bad Girls Club...where membership has its privileges!

Available wherever

is sold....

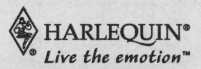

Visit us at www.eHarlequin.com

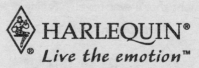

A "Mother of the Year" contest brings
overwhelming response as thousands of women
vie for the luxurious grand prize....

Kate Hoffmann

Jacqueline Diamond

Jill Shalvis

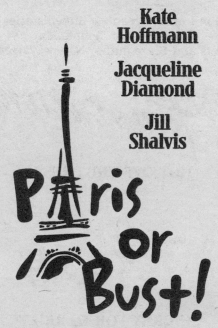

Paris or Bust!

A hilarious and romantic trio of new stories!

With a trip to Paris at stake, these women are
determined to win! But the laughs are many as three of
them discover that being finalists isn't the most
excitement they'll ever have.... Falling in love is!

Available in April 2003.

HARLEQUIN®
Makes any time special ®

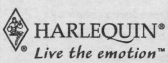

If you enjoyed what you just read,
then we've got an offer you can't resist!

Take 2 bestselling love stories FREE!

Plus get a FREE surprise gift!